The Evidence of
Things Not Seen

A contemporary novel of a family in conflict and crisis

Dr. Shawn Jones Richmond

For information contact www.DrShawnRichmond.com

Front cover photo: Dr. Shawn P. Jones Richmond
Back cover photo: Isaac Spencer Jr.

Cover design by Isaac Spencer Jr.

Published by Goshen Publishers LLC
P.O. BOX 1562
Stephens City, Va 22655

ISBN: 978-0-9994003-0-2

First Edition: September 2017
Reprinted: October 2018

10 9 8 7 6 5 4 3

Dedication

This book is dedicated to my father, Hollis R. Jones, who rests in heavenly peace, and my mother, Sarah Scott Jones, who remains my very best friend. Their personalities differ entirely from those of the fictional characters in this book; however, they passed on to me their devotion to both God and family, and that is the theme. It is also dedicated to my children who live with the freedom to choose their own paths. They inspire me.

1:   Patty

At 6:14 a.m., she reached the summit. That was 11.1 minutes longer than her best running time, so she had slowed down a little more. Her morning sprint took her up to the mountain peak daily and, despite her decrease in speed over the years, the view never disappointed. The best way to start her day, every day, was to catch the sun as it began to peek over those cascading hills.

She would take pictures there and then jot a few lines in her journal. That morning she had noted that "...the vivid autumn colors expanded for more than 100 miles painting a spectacular horizon. The seasonal scenery created a skyline that separated the earth from the sky with a breathtakingly vibrant view." Through the wide-angle camera lens, tops of trees that looked to be painted yellow and red filled the bottom, green hillsides that reflected the sunlight captured the middle, and colorful leaves captivated the top right in front of her. She could reach out and touch them and feel their morning dew. "All that beauty was captured in one awesome shot!" she wrote. She knew the splendor of the region well and anxiously awaited the colorful scene every year. Its picturesque charm made autumn her favorite season.

Her family, on the contrary, could not fathom why she left the city to move there. She couldn't succinctly articulate what drew her there either, but, whatever the attraction—it was real. It could have been the wonder of traversing the winding roads and hiking the scenic trails. It could have been that invigorating time of year when nature colored the foliage in various shades of red, orange, and yellow. Perhaps the peace and friendliness of small town communities played a part. Maybe the sprawling vineyards influenced her, too.

She packed away her journal, camera, and water bottle, and was leaving the peak to head back home when her mother telephoned. "Good morning, Patricia. How was your run?"

"It was great, Mom. I'm heading back home now."

"How was your time this morning?"

Her mother wanted to connect.

Patty fell in love with the mountains when she was in high school nearly 30 years ago and had vowed to live there again someday. Her mother hadn't.

Now she has lived there for the past 20 years. The sounds and smells, the bright leaves and active wildlife, the running springs and flowing rivers, all still amazed her. It never got old or lost its splendor.

Bored with the repetition of their phone calls, Patty didn't answer her mother's same question again. Instead, she changed the subject. "What's Dad up to?" she asked.

She had to get updates on his well-being from her mother because he and Patty were estranged. He hadn't engaged meaningfully with her since she moved away 20 years ago. Remarkably, he still hadn't gotten over it. That man carried a grudge!

Thanks to his military career, their family had been stationed in the region while Patty was a teenager. Her memories of the area were much more pleasant than his. When he retired and she graduated high school, they moved back to New York, hurriedly. Her brother Lewis still had one year of high school to complete. He had to transfer high schools in his senior year and graduate in New York because they were not staying one minute longer past Dad's retirement. That had been the parents' plan all along.

Patty had earned track and field scholarships and could have remained in the Shenandoah Mountains, but her Dad insisted that she go back north with them for college. She did as he asked and attended New York State University. She called that her first regret.

In college, she had desperately hoped to make the Olympic team. Her timing was good enough and her coaches were confident that she could qualify. Her roommate, Ida, believed in her as well and they all encouraged her. When she put on her red and white uniform, pulled her hair back into a loose ponytail, and focused on that finish line, no one on their team could out-sprint her. There was one limiting factor: her Dad was not supportive of the idea. He did not see a future for her as an athlete and, therefore, insisted that she not waste time training and trying out for the Olympics. She conceded. He approved her participation on the college team, but forbade her to compete globally. Dad had spoken, so she again did as he ordered and did not race beyond her collegiate team. That became her second regret.

Her undergraduate grade point average was solid, but it was her track and field performance that earned her a full-ride scholarship to graduate school. Her Dad insisted that she continue at NYSU because they had an outstanding Master of Business Administration program. She would have preferred to study Natural Science or Physical Education, but he demanded she obtain an MBA. No one, anywhere, ever, spoke up against him and she certainly did not either. Well, not at that time anyway. Patty continued at NYSU for another three years, gave up completely on her dream of becoming an Olympian, and earned her MBA. Her coach and teammates were again disappointed. Her roommate was disheartened. She was saddened. That regretful decision made strike three.

Her Dad, however, was proud. Patty was their first child to get an MBA. Trailing along just one year behind her, Lewis followed that designated path as well. It was not what either of them desired, but the accomplishments pleased their Dad.

"He's in his office working on a sermon for this week," her Mom said, still on their phone call. "Would you like to speak with him?" She always sounded so formal when she spoke of him, more like his personal assistant than his wife and life partner. Not just when it came to her Dad, but in general, Patty's Mom seemed to function without emotion. Patty often wondered what created such a void in her that made her at times seem robotic, always polite and pleasant, but mechanical.

"No, Ma'am. I've got to go. Talk to you later, Mom?"

"Sure, Patricia," she said apathetically. She had tried relentlessly over the years to help them reconcile and hadn't given up yet, but her expectations were not very high.

When Patty finished the MBA program, her Dad had pulled strings to get her a job on Wall Street. She thought it was some CEO of a Fortune 500 company who attended his church, but she didn't pay enough attention to catch all the details. She hadn't applied for that position and did not want it. Throughout college and grad school, she had made it clear to her parents that she did not like life in New York. It just wasn't for her.

Fortunately, an opportunity presented for her to teach at the community college in Shenandoah. That was her ticket back home and away from the traffic, congestion, intensity, expenses, and all that comprised urban life. Out of respect for his authority, or fear of his rebuke, she had spent seven years there for college and grad school—that was more than plenty. Lewis shared her sentiment, but he would not dare speak up against their father, so he remained there working on Wall Street as their Dad strongly suggested.

Patty often sensed that her mom disagreed with their lack of input regarding their careers, but she never spoke up. Patty wished her mom had been more vocal when he ordered them against their wishes—and even more so when he alienated Patty. She couldn't tell, because of her mom's unresponsiveness, that the dissension in the family bothered her. Her mom wanted desperately to settle the discord. The challenge was that all her attempts at reconciling their relationship had been futile because they required Patty to compromise again—to deny the life that she wanted, again—to appease him. She wouldn't. She couldn't.

"Love you, Mom. Have a good day."

"Patricia, he means well."

"Mom, it's been 20 years. He really needs to get over it."

The chip on his shoulder appeared when they first learned of Patty's career decision. She had applied for it, prayed about it, and longed for it so badly that when she received her Offer of Employment letter, she did not have to think about whether not she'd accept. She did not consult anyone—not even Lewis who, she was certain, quietly cheered her bravery, but like Mom, he would not have spoken against their dad.

There was, decidedly, nothing to ponder, nothing to contemplate, and nothing to discuss. They did not have a say in Patty's decision to take the job and move to her beloved Virginia. Her dad was disapproving, to put it mildly.

Patty had kept the entire process a secret from them, including when she'd left town to interview. Ida was aware, of course. She only informed them, not asked, when it was official. She actually had received the job offer and was holding it in her hand. Being slightly afraid of his reaction, she didn't drive over to their place to tell her dad. She had called and asked her mom to put her on speakerphone.

It had been 20 years and yet she still remembered every word and emotion of that phone call—

***

Dad was outraged, "Patricia, are you serious? No one has ever heard of that little school. It's in the middle of nowhere."

"It's a beautiful place, Dad."

"The salary will not compare to Wall Street. Not even close."

She was calm, "Yes, Sir. The wage is a little lower than some of the other job offers I received, especially those on Wall Street."

"But you'll work just as hard for less money and you'll be alone there, won't you?"

She answered, surprisingly with no quiver in her voice. For the first time in her life, she was speaking up for what she wanted, "Yes, Sir. Faculty members work hard and, yes, I do not have family in the area."

"Then why are you doing this, Patricia?" he shouted.

"I want to live there. I can't explain it any other way, Dad. I want to live there." Her voice was steady and her tone was respectful, but stern.

She remembered wondering, if a little confidence felt so good, why had it taken her so long to try it? Her dad was a Lieutenant General in the United States Marine Corp. He was also a renowned preacher. That surely explained his intimidation tactics and commanding approach with the people in his life, including his own family. He had always commanded with directives, instead of discussing their family matters. That had been their way of life. It just wasn't effective with Patty anymore.

It still worked with Lewis though. NYSU was their parents' alma mater, the place where they met and studied, and they had insisted that their children follow tradition. They did. Patty had hoped that her actions would have broken the cycle and set an example for Lewis to pursue his own dreams. Never disobedient, when his dad insisted that Lewis accept a Wall Street opportunity, he did. Two decades later, he still worked there.

"Patricia, if you are determined to move there, to that uncivilized place, to a forest, against my wishes, please know that you will be on your own. If you defy me, I will not support you." Her dad's threat was clear.

For Patty, his opinion of Shenandoah was irrelevant. She didn't need his approval and respectfully said, "I understand, Dad."

He ended the call without saying "goodbye" or "I love you." He just hung up.

***

Moving on. She immediately accepted the job offer. She would have agreed to work just about any job that allowed her to live in this gorgeous expanse again. She decided she would figure out her budget, adjust it where necessary, and find a way to live happily on a modest income—without her dad's support.

That one phone call set the tone for the next 20 years of their relationship. Of course, she had longed for them to mend. She yearned for reconciliation. Occasionally, she invited them to visit from New York. Lewis would come and so would her best friend Ida. Her dad, however, would always decline which, of course, meant that her mom couldn't come either.

She never stopped loving them, so a couple of times a year she would visit them in their home, on their terms. She didn't mind the trip to New York because she always knew that after a quick stay with them, she would return to her lovely little home here in the mountains.

The last time she invited them was a few months ago. She was hosting a birthday party for Estelle, a co-worker who shared her mom's birthday. It would have been fun for them to celebrate together, so she called her dad.

"Dad, I was thinking about Mom's birthday. I'd love to have a dinner party for her," she started.

"Where?" he asked. "There, in your little house?" he belted out as if insulted. His tone implied that her home would be inadequate for hosting a dinner for her mom.

It is true that for most people, hers would not be considered a dream house. Unlike her parents' home, there was neither metropolitan skyrise view nor uniformed doorman, no marble foyer, and no grand façade. There was not much about her little place that would make anyone daydream of the life inside. In fact, the inside was even less remarkable. Within its small space, there were no modern stainless steel appliances, no custom-made granite counters, and no oversized bathtubs.

Her home was a modest cabin in the mountains. The porch expanded the full width of the house with two huge picture windows on the front—one at either end. Tall oak trees surrounded it, almost hiding it from the main road. It was the farthest thing from the Wall Street condominium that her dad had selected for her, but she loved it.

It was *her* dream home. She had dreamt of it for years, since high school, and every morning that she awakened here she gave thanks. She adored it then and still cherishes it now, her charming 1200 square feet of loveliness.

She answered him, "Yes, Sir. Here in my home. I think she'd enjoy herself. You might like it too. It's peaceful, a great place to escape the city and relax. I could show you around. Things have changed since you were stationed here. You could meet a few of my friends." She knew that she was hoping against all odds. He had never been interested in meeting the people in her life there.

Most of her local friends were natives of the region. Since the early 1700s it had been home to Iroquois, a family of North American Indians. It has been said that five tribes of nations once inhabited the land, each speaking some dialect of the Iroquois. She'd learned some of the language from her friends that she wished he would meet.

"I can relax at home," he said and then belligerently added, "and I don't need to meet the deer people or watch for bears."

Having lived there years ago, her dad knew the history of the region. He knew that the name Shenandoah came from the Iroquoian word for "deer." He also knew that she had bonded with a native family, The Goodleafs, when she was in high school. He never cared to meet them or learn of their culture, but she did, and they welcomed her back when she returned after graduate school. She loved so much about them and they included her in all their family functions, celebrations, and meals. They had a way of storytelling that was fascinating. And many of their philosophies shaped her lifestyle.

He had mentioned the black bears because he knew they were plentiful, numbering as many as 6,000. She saw them frequently in the summer and autumn. They ventured up into trees and almost anywhere else in search of food for their binge that preceded their yearly winter hibernation. She had learned a few tricks such as bungee cording her garbage cans to lessen their attraction to the bears and to keep repellant in her running pack.

She also relied on Rosie, her Beagle, to alert her when bears were near. She'd rise up on her hind feet, threw her head back, and release long, loud howls when Patty was not yet cleared to go to and from her truck. She'd also howl if their presence meant that it was time for Patty to end her nap out under her portico that replaced her back porch.

"OK, Dad," she conceded, "I'll just plan to drive up for Mom's birthday. No problem."

"Roger that," he said and hung up. In the beginning, his abrupt endings to their phone calls hurt her feelings. Twenty years later she was immune to his indignation.

Having finished her phone call with her mom and reflected on her relationship with her dad, she was still heading back down the mountain and almost home. She always felt peaceful after those meditative moments of hiking, photographing, and journaling on the mountain peak. Her photographs were actually pretty good for a novice. She'd selected some of them, the most spectacular sunrises and sunsets, to backdrop the invitations for her upcoming event.

The sunrises were so alluring that she never needed an alarm clock to wake her in time to catch them. Her body, mind, and soul were instinctively aroused to wake up in time to pour her first cup of coffee and jog up a trail to catch the sunrise. Rosie knew that once the coffee was poured and consumed, she also could look forward to their morning jog.

On their way back home that morning, Rosie began to chase a squirrel. With her huge floppy ears flapping in the wind and her long white tail standing straight up in the air, she moved quickly and determinedly.

"Rosie, Rosie, come back girl!" Patty called for her.

Patty could hear Rosie barking and her feet rustling the leaves on the ground, but the sounds were fading as she ran farther away. Not only was Rosie too old to catch the squirrels anymore, but she couldn't always hear well either. She, too, was a little older now.

Those quests were fun for Rosie but often frustrated Patty who realized that Rosie had hunting instincts and was naturally inclined to wander off. It was just at the most inconvenient times that Rosie would venture so far that she couldn't hear Patty calling for her. She'd get lost and Patty would have to go and find her.

Patty was calling her that morning, "Rosie, Rosie, where are you girl?" but couldn't hear her. As much as Patty liked Rosie to have freedom, Patty thought about purchasing a leash for her. Patty just reviled the idea of Rosie being tethered or restricted in any way.

When Patty finally found Rosie and saw her running back, she checked the time and she needed to get ready for work. She was expecting news that day.

2:   Retirement

Finally, back home, Patty had her usual quick breakfast: instant oatmeal with homemade applesauce mixed in for flavor. Then she showered and dressed in less than half an hour. The college dress code for faculty was business casual, so she didn't have to wear anything fancy. She wouldn't want to anyway. Her uncluttered closet had sufficient sweaters and shawls for the season. She matched a dark brown sweater and wrap with a long tan skirt, and tall brown riding boots.

Her clothes were always loose fitting and she imagined most people would be surprised to know that there was an incredibly fit body underneath—an athlete's body. She preferred her understated, gypsy-like clothing because it was comfortable. She would admit though, that her wardrobe left plenty of room for an infusion of fashion updates. Ida had tried over the years to style her well, but she always reverted back to comfort and convenience soon after they parted ways.

She also saved time from primping and adorning in her bathroom. Her hair was pulled back into either a ponytail or a topknot bun. She reserved makeup and fancy hair-dos for rare, very special occasions. She just wasn't willing to commit 25 minutes of her mornings to cosmetics, not to mention the adjustments to her budget for beauty products. She wore her favorite pair of gold hoop earrings, a birthday gift from Ida last year, and a beautiful gold watch that was a Christmas gift from Lewis a few years earlier. All set, she'd made sure there was food and water out for Rosie and then headed off to work.

As soon as she got into her truck that morning, Ida called so they could chat for a few minutes on her drive to work. She usually arrived on campus by 7:30 a.m., half an hour before her first class began.

"Good morning!" Ida began. "How was your run?"

"It was OK. I got a few great pictures of the sunrise, but Rosie ran off again. How are you?"

Her voice was pleasant and, like many New Yorkers, her speech was fast. In one breath she said, "I'm good. I remembered that you get news today and wanted to wish you luck. You know I'll be thinking about you and can't wait to hear what happened."

"Thanks, Ida," she said. She could always count on her for encouragement.

They chatted until Patty pulled into the parking lot on campus. "I'll call you tonight and fill you in," Patty told Ida before they hung up.

Patty had a ritual in her classroom of praying and worshipping before her workday began. She had just arrived that morning when Estelle entered her classroom. It was not out of the ordinary for her to be on campus early, but she only visited faculty in their classrooms for serious matters. Estelle was the Director of the Office of Faculty Retirement; Patty had been anticipating a response on her application.

"Good morning, Patty," Estelle greeted.

Estelle's smile was always so bright that it illuminated the room and it seemed to have some sweet secret concealed behind it. She was the same age as Patty's parents and was classically beautiful like her mother. She wore her hair in an upsweep with light bangs and most days she wore knee-length dresses with low heels. Her makeup would have been understated except that she loved her ruby red lipstick.

"Hey, Estelle. What a pleasant surprise," Patty said to her.

Estelle hugged Patty the way that a mother lovingly embraces her child. "Pleasant indeed. I have good news."

Estelle had come to inform Patty that her request had been approved. Estelle congratulated Patty, presented her retirement package, and discussed the outbound process.

With excitement, Patty reached to accept the documents that Estelle was handing her. "This is great news, Estelle. Thank you."

She was genuinely concerned about Patty's decision and was still smiling when she caringly asked, "Patty, baby, are you sure about this?"

Patty assured her, "Yes, Ma'am. I am."

Estelle recalled with great detail the first day that Patty came to work at Shen Valley Community College. She was on the welcome committee and helped Patty get acclimated. She never hid the fact that she was proud of Patty. If asked, not that anyone would, Estelle could've recounted Patty's accolades over the past two decades from memory. That's why the visit that morning, the official notification from the Shen Valley Community College Office of Faculty Retirement, was also personal for them.

In many ways, Estelle had mentored, coached, and nurtured Patty. In the absence of Patty's own mother for the past 20 years, there was a bond between them and, while not explicable, most definitely a familial connection.

With a quick check of the time, Patty was cognizant of how she needed to get to her prayer before the students arrived. She had to wrap up that conversation. "Thanks again, Estelle. See you at lunch?"

When Estelle saw Patty glance over at the clock on her desk, she knew as well that they would have to continue their conversation later. "Sure," she said, "and I'll have our lunch warm in the lounge. Same time, right?"

"Yes, Ma'am. Same time. I always look forward to it."

She only had a few minutes remaining, so her prayer was brief. She was able to cover the essentials though. She gave thanks for family and friends, sought guidance in life planning, and requested protection from harm. She couldn't explain the emotion that she felt during her morning prayers recently, but something was different—unsettling. It had been happening for several weeks.

Patty was relieved when she finished just before her first of 25 students arrived. They didn't know about her habitual mornings in the classroom because she never told anyone other than Ida. Although, she was sure that over the years, on more than one occasion, she glanced up and glimpsed Estelle just outside her classroom door. Neither of them had ever mentioned it.

When she opened her bag to put her retirement package in it, she saw the party invitations that she had been designing. She was hand-making an artistically unique card for each guest and hoped they'd appreciate their keepsakes. She put a different sunrise picture, one she had personally taken, on the front of each invitation, a handwritten note inside, and a special print of a sunset on the back. She also hand-painted colorful, autumnal leaves across the bottom of each envelope. She had begun working on them several weeks prior when she'd first submitted her retirement request.

The package from Estelle was thorough and Patty was sure it contained useful resources, but those weeks pending official approval had provided ample time for her to plan her next life chapter. She had already calculated her finances, researched her insurance options, and assured her future stability. She hadn't packed up her classroom yet because she would work for another couple of months and would need her teaching aids, books, and lesson plans to finish that semester in December successfully.

At the end of the day, when she was on her way home from work, she called Ida.

"Well? How'd it go? Did you get news? Are you retiring?" she asked anxiously.

"I'm retiring in December, Ida. They approved my request."

"Congrats! You don't sound excited. How do you feel?" She was so intuitive.

"I'm excited." Patty searched for the words. "I really appreciate Estelle's thoughtfulness. She asked if I were sure about this and she seemed troubled."

"Well," she said, "she's always loved you like a daughter, Patty. It's only natural that she'd be worried a little."

"True," Patty responded, "but she's concerned and..." Patty tried to explain, "... and lately in my morning prayers in the classroom, I get this feeling. It's like I'm nervous or anxious."

"Do you think it's about your retirement or something else?"

"I don't know." Patty suddenly became uncharacteristically emotional.

"Oh no. What is it? Are you OK?" Ida asked.

"Yes, I'm OK. I think it's just anxiety."

"Keep praying," Ida said, "and I'll be in agreement with you."

"Thanks, Ida."

"No worries. Everything will be fine. You'll see."

Patty had just pulled her SUV into her driveway and saw Rosie waiting out on their front porch. She came running up to greet her.

"I'm home, Ida. We'll talk later?"

"Sure. Talk to you later."

Walking up the sidewalk toward her front door, she stopped briefly to pet Rosie and admire her little cottage in the woods. She questioned herself, *How silly is it to be upset about something that hasn't happened yet and when you don't even know what it is?* She had decided to pull herself together and shake that uneasy feeling.

Later that evening she didn't have much of an appetite, so she skipped dinner and went for a short walk with Rosie. The plan was to use that hike to sort out her mixed emotions. She was happy to be retiring from teaching and excited about her future plans. So, what was up with the internal warning system sounding off and alarming? How could she have been panicky about something she couldn't see? It wasn't until she finally made it back to her portico swing with Rosie late that evening that she started to feel better. She shifted her focus back to her retirement and called Ida.

"Ida, I have decided to have my retirement party sooner. I won't wait until December. In fact, I've already designed the invitations. I still have to teach through the end of this semester, but I don't feel like I should delay the celebration. Couldn't I have my party sooner?"

"Of course you could. We only need a couple of weeks to plan it." Patty was relieved that Ida was on board.

"Who will you invite?" she asked.

"Well, I'm thinking there's no better way to capstone my career than to have the people I love, despite our dysfunction, gather at the home I love, and in the season that I love most."

"I'm not surprised," she said.

"It's been 20 years, Ida. I'm moving on to something new and I'm excited. I don't need Dad's approval, but," Patty was searching for the words. "I'm tired of the dissension, so I'll invite them here, again."

Ida understood Patty's dilemma, "I know, my friend. Just tell me what I can do." Her response was assuring.

"Let's plan this party."

Patty was still out back on her swinging bench with the oversized cushions and her heart rate was calming. She didn't have to explain herself to Ida. She was just always down for whatever.

The portico pointed Patty toward the sunsets with perfect aim. She always left her tripod set up so all she had to do was set her camera on it and set its timer. Nature took care of the rest. She checked and, sure enough, the camera was capturing the sunset.

Ida answered, "OK. Let's do it. Let me pour a glass of wine and grab my tablet. Hold on."

"Me too," Patty said and laid her phone down, "I'll be right back."

Her evenings were usually capped with wine from one of the local vineyards. Her mood and her palette determined if she chose red or white. Her preferred Chardonnay had an aroma of pears and a hint of butterscotch, but she more often chose a red: a medium dry, light wine. That's what she poured during their phone call that evening. Her favorite red—an aged Cabernet with a trace of oak that provided balance and flavor—she only opened for special occasions. She planned to serve that at her party.

"I'm back," Ida said.

"Me too."

It did not take them long to decide on the biggest details of when and where. It would be at her home in a few weeks: the first Saturday in November.

They continued to plan over the next couple of days until they covered all the particulars. They had decided on the decorations, the food, and the music. Patty would set up a banquet table in her living room. They wouldn't need a caterer. They began cooking together in college and still enjoyed it, so they'd make the food. The surrounding foliage and flora, once gathered and arranged, would make the perfect table centerpiece. Estelle would gladly take care of that.

They also decided to borrow a piano from the school music room and Estelle would play it after dinner. She had trained classically for years and would select her best pieces to showcase. Estelle also gave private lessons, free of charge, to a few of the locals. Patty was one of Estelle's students. The party guests were sure to enjoy their melodious duet.

Her invitations went out with short notice, arriving about two weeks before the party, because it took her so long to hand-make them. She was sure that all the guests would understand, though. She had called them to let them know that their invitations were being mailed. All were local except for her parents, her brother, and Ida, who were all in New York.

The Sunday before the party she was on the phone reviewing the final details with Ida.

"So, how many RSVPs do we have remaining?" Ida asked.

"Let's see." Patty began counting. "My parents have not confirmed either way yet. Neither has Lewis, but he hasn't been feeling well. I'll call them again this week. Everyone else has responded, including the Goodleafs."

"The Goodleafs? Your neighbors? I'll finally get to meet them. They're always busy or away when I visit. Their vineyard is my favorite."

"Yes, and they have offered as much wine as we'd like."

"Cool. I'll be bringing some home with me." She took wine back to New York with her every year. "And apples?" she added. "I love the apples from their orchards."

The Goodleaf Orchard and Winery had been in their family for several generations and they knew how much the community enjoyed their products. They had taught most of their neighbors, including Patty, how to make applesauce and apple cider vinegar. They also generously supplied wine for special events such as Patty's upcoming retirement celebration.

She had finished checking off names on the guest list when she mentioned Ida's name. "And you, Ida Wilson, you'll be here." She couldn't wait to see her.

Ida answered in that loving tone and rapid speech, "Patty, it's only a four-hour drive from New York to Shenandoah. Nothing short of a catastrophe will keep me away from your retirement party."

"Thanks, Ida. Love you."

"Love you, too. Bye-bye."

3:   Lewis

He needed to return his sister's call about her upcoming retirement party in Shenandoah. He had been a little under the weather and was not sure he could make the drive, but did not want to disappoint her. He had hoped that his condition would not interfere with his work the past weekend. He'd confirmed his schedule, received the deposit payment, and checked his equipment.

Over the past 20 years, he'd never canceled a photography job and that weekend was no different. He worked at a wedding rehearsal in Manhattan on Friday night. He conducted a site check to make sure that he planned the proper lighting, lenses, and angles required to photograph their wedding the following day. He had done that hundreds of times over the past two decades and the satisfaction of working with people to capture their memories had never diminished at all.

His parents gave him his first camera for his 16th birthday. True to their nature, it was top of the line and was really a high-end camera for a novice. He had wanted a camera for a while and was excited to finally get one despite his dad's delivery.

"Junior," he hated when he called him that, "this is a Konica C35 AF, the world's first production autofocus camera. You just point and shoot. You don't have to be very skilled. You can get good pictures from it for a long time if you take care of it."

"Yes, Sir. Thank you."

He did just that and photographed everything at his school—his friends, sporting events, club meetings, the buildings, the gym, and even the buses. He didn't stop with their school though. Because the family was stationed in the Shenandoah Valley, he also photographed nature, the mountains, and the wildlife.

He and his sister Patty would venture off to find the best places to get great pictures. She didn't have a camera, so he'd share his with her. They took turns shooting pictures. She was athletic, a track star, so they'd point to a spot and he'd time her while she ran to it as fast as she could, always aiming to break her own record. He would photograph her sprinting because she was so fast and graceful and she loved it so much.

Photography was his favorite hobby all through college and graduate school. While in college, he worked part-time and saved enough money to purchase a professional digital camera, a Nikon F-3, with a 1.3 megapixel sensor—the same model used by photojournalists. The day he bought that camera ranked among the best days he'd ever had. That upgrade was the first of many. Today, he uses the highest-end cameras from Samsung, Nikon, and Canon. He selected the camera, lenses, and lighting based on the nature of the event and the type of pictures his clients wanted.

Had he been given a choice, he would have chosen to be a professional photojournalist. He still dreamt of the chance to capture images in order to tell a news story.

No such choice existed. His father did not, would not, consent because he didn't see how it would have provided a secure, steady income.

His father knew that Lewis could only afford college with his support and he would not agree to fund his education unless he agreed to become a businessman. Both their parents had MBAs and, in their opinions, that was a more reputable, stable profession. They would not approve of any school other than NYSU and no career other than an MBA. So, Patty and Lewis had both followed suit.

Photojournalism remained his passion, but his job on Wall Street demanded all of his time on weekdays leaving only weekends for his hobby. He mostly shot weddings because they did not require travel or interfere with his job schedule. He'd learned to make wedding photography as fulfilling as photojournalism and he was pretty good at it. He got to use his cameras. He met great people. He made extra money. It was not his dream career, but he remained grateful for every event he got to work.

Last weekend's job was no different. It thrilled him to partake in a special event, capture it perfectly, and see the rewarding look of delight on his clients' faces when they viewed the pictures. He took pictures that told their love story from engagement to wedding to first child.

He wished he had felt a little better that weekend. His cough had not been painful, even though it was persistent and annoying. It was distracting at the wedding rehearsal that Friday evening. Even if he could have ignored it, the wedding party could not. He apologized to them and tried to be less disruptive. It had lingered for weeks and definitely merited medical attention, but he was sure that it wasn't serious enough for a visit to the hospital emergency room. He planned to call his doctor for an appointment on Monday. For the time being though, he just needed to press through that weekend's work and take pictures that would do the lovely and highly profiled couple proud.

After the rehearsal, he stopped by the drugstore again to ask the pharmacist about cough medications. Unfortunately, he'd already purchased all of her recommendations: the syrups, the lozenges, the powders, and the pills. None had provided relief. She strongly recommended that he see a doctor, and he planned to, after the wedding. For that weekend, however, he just continued to sample from his over-the-counter cough suppressants.

On Saturday, the medicines helped while he photographed the wedding. He admitted, though, that it was dangerous to mix from the overabundance of medications and the combination did make him a little groggy. One of the wedding guests had noticed and approached him to ask if he were well.

"Hello, Lewis."

"Hello."

"You don't remember me?"

"I'm sorry."

"You photographed my niece's engagement party and wedding. You've actually done several events for our family. We deem you the family photographer. This bride," he pointed to the front of the venue, is also my niece, my brother's other daughter. If you don't mind me asking, are you OK? You don't look well."

Lewis told him that he had a persistent cough and that he was attempting to treat it at home.

"Are you under a doctor's care?" he asked.

"Not really. It takes a while to get an appointment with my doctor and since it's just a cough I'm trying over-the-counter meds first."

"How long has this been persisting?" he asked.

"Weeks, several weeks maybe. Actually, now that I think about it, possibly a couple of months."

He handed Lewis his card and said, "I'm an internal medical doctor. If you call my office first thing on Monday, I'm sure I can fit you in and run a few tests for you."

"Wow. That's kind of you. Thanks. I'll call first thing Monday."

He smiled a really cute smile and said, "Don't thank me yet. You haven't received my bill."

Lewis thought the gentleman winked at him just as he was walking away. It made him smile.

After the wedding Saturday night, Lewis was pleased to view the photos. He had gotten some great shots, which meant that the couple would not be disappointed. Therein, lay his fear—

disappointing someone who was counting on him. He recognized it and knew where it came from, of course. He just hadn't done much to address it.

Gratified with the weekend's wedding photos, he spent Sunday morning searching the internet for home remedies. Patty's retirement party was just days away and there must have been something to alleviate his coughing so he could travel and attend it. The most promising solution seemed to have been the honey, lemon, cayenne pepper, and ginger recipe, so he gave it a try. He mixed it with green tea, added a shot of Irish whiskey, and sipped until he finished a full mug, just before falling to sleep again. To his chagrin, when he woke up, that remedy also was failing. He just had to get through one more night with the nagging, annoying, and now painful, cough and then he'd call the new doctor.

Before passing out again, he sent a quick text to his assistant, asking her to clear his calendar of appointments on Monday. The firm frowned upon calling in sick, so he never had, but he really needed to see a doctor. As always, she replied to him immediately, even on a Sunday night, "It's about time, Lewis. Feel better soon."

He didn't use alarm clocks because his body awakened automatically in response to the sunrise. It had been that way for as long as he could remember. That's why it was so strange that when Monday morning finally came and he awakened, half the morning was already past. He had overslept, possibly for the first time ever.

He reached for his tan leather jacket, the one he wore to the wedding Saturday. Surprisingly, it was not hanging in his closet. He had thrown it over the back of his armchair and that was uncharacteristic of him. His weathered, dark brown, leather fedora hat was on the floor. As far back as he could recall, he was trained to hang up jackets and hats as soon as he arrived home. When growing up, his father conducted random bedroom inspections and everything had to have been found in order. If there were disorder, there was consequences.

Maybe he was more than just a little groggy from the medications. He reached into his jacket pocket for the card that he received from the cute doctor at the wedding, *Gary Goldstein, M.D.*, and dialed his office phone number.

"Good morning," Lewis pleasantly greeted. "I'm Lewis Harris. I'd like an appointment with Dr. Gary Goldstein, please."

"Yes, sir, Mr. Harris," from a kind voice on the phone, "The doctor has been expecting your call. How soon can you come in this morning?"

He actually hadn't thought about that yet either. He had to re-read the business card for his office address and then estimate how long would it take him to dress and catch an Uber across town. Too much cough medicine, maybe? "Um, I can be there in about an hour and a half, maybe two hours."

"That'll work, Mr. Harris."

"Great. Thank you."

With that scheduled, he rushed to shower and dress. His Wall Street career required conservative suits and neckties, and for photographing weddings he usually wore the same. On the rare occasions when he wasn't working, he took the liberty to dabble with more chic couture. He wished he could have worn his favorite designers' clothing every day, mixing and matching colors, prints, and textures.

Surprisingly, he struggled with an outfit for that morning. There was actually a slight panic overtaking him as he contemplated what to wear to the doctor's office. Where was that coming from? It was just a doctor's appointment, right?

He finally decided on his distressed John Elliott slim jeans and a tan Valentino studded-collar shirt. That would work with his Ami Alexandre Mattiussi brown leather jacket, brown fedora hat, and tan Gucci shoes. For a little more autumn style, he added a Gucci scarf and matching sunglasses too.

He could not believe how much time he had taken to select, lay out, and try on clothes. He still had to shave and shower, charge his cell phone battery, because he hadn't done that since before the wedding a couple of days ago, and he needed to eat something before his appointment.

He made it down to his building lobby and greeted the doorman just as his Uber arrived.

"Good morning, Mr. Harris," the Uber driver greeted him as he got into his car. "How are you this morning?"

"Well enough," Lewis said and still somewhat unorganized, "but I'm running a little behind on my way to a doctor's appointment."

"I understand. We'll get there quickly. I know this route well."

"I really hate to ask but I could use a couple of favors."

"Sure, what can I do for you?"

"Well, could I plug in my phone to charge?"

"Sure," he answered.

"And, do you mind terribly if I eat my oatmeal in your car?"

"Not at all, Sir. Please enjoy."

"Thanks. And if I should fall asleep on the way…"

He interrupted, "… no worries. I'll wake you when we get there."

"I really appreciate it."

He was a reliable driver and woke Lewis when they arrived at Dr. Goldstein's office. Lewis assumed that he had passed out quickly because he didn't recall anything from the ride. He still hadn't eaten. He hadn't charged his phone either but the driver had done it for him. He was grateful for the kindness the driver showed him that morning.

"Have a great day," Lewis said as he exited the car.

"You too and enjoy Shenandoah."

"Thanks" and he shut the door. Interesting, he thought, I don't remember mentioning Shenandoah to him.

He took the elevator up to Dr. Goldstein's office on the 49th floor. There were several other patients in his reception area, flipping through magazines, swiping screens on their cell phones, and watching the news on the wall-mounted television across the room. Lewis wondered how long he'd have to wait to be worked in and if he could stay awake long enough. Within minutes after he checked in, his name was called to go back to an examination room. He was still feeling a little woozy and his cough was relentless, so he was really hoping the doctor could prescribe something to help him.

One of the nurses asked him about his symptoms as she checked and recorded his vital signs. She was saying something about using a mobile app, but he couldn't really concentrate for very long that morning. He couldn't even stay awake for the entire examination.

He must have dozed off again for a few minutes because the next thing he recalled was Dr. Goldstein waving some sort of small flashlight back-and-forth between his eyes.

"Mr. Harris? Mr. Harris? Can you hear me?" Dr. Goldstein was asking.

"Yes."

"Are you injured, Mr. Harris?"

"Huh? I'm sorry, what?"

He explained, "Mr. Harris, you may have passed out. Do you know where you are?"

He was leaning in closely and Lewis could see two other people in the room, but could not make out who they were. He could see the doctor clearly, though. He wore a white lab jacket over a starchy white shirt with a skinny red tie. His olive skin was perfectly smooth and his large nose curved downward toward his soft chin. Lewis guessed he was Jewish American. He had dark hair with flecks of grey and he was clean-shaven which revealed those darn dimples and that bright smile. He could also smell him and thought, *my goodness his cologne smells so good.*

Lewis answered him, "Yes, I'm in Dr. Goldstein's office."

"Very good," he replied. "We have a wheelchair here and we will be taking you downstairs into another office for x-rays, a CT scan, and an MRI. That will give us an idea of what might be going on with your brain and lungs."

"That seems reasonable," Lewis said, "Thank you." Did he say *brain and lungs?* Examining his lungs was understandable because of the cough, but why would he need to examine his brain?

"You're welcome. By the time those scans are completed we should have the results back from your blood work."

"OK," Lewis acknowledged but didn't recall them drawing blood.

He appreciated Dr. Goldstein's thorough approach to his diagnosis, but he was a relatively healthy man so it may have been excessive. He was thinking that his coughing spells might have just been symptomatic of a respiratory infection.

He was taken downstairs for the additional tests and must have fallen asleep again because a nurse had come in to tell him that he was all done and his results would be in the following day.

"I was told upstairs that I could check them on the mobile app. Should I do that tomorrow?" he asked her.

She said, "Maybe. It depends though. Sometimes, GG, likes to speak with his patients and explain the results first."

"I'm sorry. Who's GG?" he asked.

She said, "Oh. Sorry. Yes, we all call Dr. Goldstein, GG. He prefers it. He and his twin brother, Harry, are both doctors in Manhattan. Their nicknames distinguish one Dr. Goldstein from the other."

"I see. Are they identical twins?" He was not sure why he asked. God could not have blessed mankind with two of them.

"No, they are fraternal. Their personalities are opposite also. GG is liberal and more relaxed and informal, while Dr. Harry is orthodox and very reserved. Both are excellent doctors so you're in good hands." She smiled.

"So, shall I call his office in the morning?"

"Yes," she said, "and here are a few instructions in the meantime."

She reviewed the list with him, but he didn't remember everything she said. GG, what a cute nickname, recommended that he refrain from taking any more over-the-counter medications, drink plenty of fluids, and plan to take a few days off from work. Being done there, he arranged for his Uber home and left the doctor's office, without getting to see him again that day.

After he arrived home, coincidentally, with the same Uber driver, he made another cup of the tea concoction and wondered what the test results would reveal. Perhaps there was a simple explanation for the coughing and the blackouts.

Tuesday morning came quickly. For the second consecutive day, he overslept. What was going on? How could he have slept half the morning away, again? He scrambled for his phone to call and get the test results.

"Good morning, GG. How are you?"

"I'm well, Mr. Harris. How are you feeling?"

"Please call me Lewis," he insisted.

"OK," he chuckled, "Lewis, how are you feeling?"

"I think I'm OK. I'm just sleeping a lot between the coughing spells."

"Right. Your test results are in and I'd like to go over them with you."

"Great. I'm listening."

"I think in person will be best."

"Do I need to come to your office?"

"Yes. That's a good idea."

"OK. I'll head on over." He dressed and took another Uber over, same driver again, and was wondering why GG didn't just explain the results over the phone.

When he arrived, just as the day before, he did not have to wait to see the doctor. There was a tiny conference room with no tables and only two armchairs filling the space. He had only been seated there for a couple of minutes when GG entered looking concerned. His nurse nodded at Lewis as if she were consoling him when she handed him a tablet and then closed the door when she exited. He wasn't prepared.

He didn't feel great but he wasn't expecting those results. He wasn't even worried until GG mentioned an immediate biopsy. He took care to explain the surgical procedure and was using many terms with which Lewis was not familiar. He'd have to search them on the internet later: *pneumonic obstructions, metastasis, cranial inflammation, advanced stage 4.*

While GG was explaining the results, Lewis received a call from Patty. Her timing was great and he welcomed the interruption because he actually needed a break from GG's explanations.

"Hi Patty. What's up?"

"Hey Lewis. Feeling better?"

"A little. I received your invitation. Thanks."

"Can you come?"

"Of course," he said. "I wouldn't miss it for the world. I'm in a meeting right now though. Can I call you later?"

"Sure. I love you, Lewis."

"Love you too, Sis. Bye."

That call had been a great diversion. Then he started coughing again, violently. GG handed him tissue and pointed toward his face. He stood to look in the mirror that was hanging on the wall by the door and saw that he had coughed up blood.

GG began to speak again. "Lewis, I know this is a lot to process. Do you have any questions for me?"

"Yes," he answered, "How soon do I need to schedule this biopsy?"

"The sooner the better, Lewis."

"My sister wants me to come to her retirement celebration this weekend. I'm going."

"We could get your biopsy done tomorrow. I've already contacted my brother, Harry, and he has an opening in his schedule. It's an in-and-out procedure so you'd go home the same day."

"Will I be OK to drive by Friday?" Lewis asked. "Her party is Saturday."

"I doubt that, Lewis. You'll probably be undergoing treatment that will prohibit driving. Where does your sister live?"

"In the Shenandoah Valley. It's about a 4-hour drive."

"You're kidding me. I'm going there this weekend for an annual wine festival. It's a big deal for my aunt and her neighbors, so I go to support them every year. While I'm there I always get to stock up from my favorite wineries."

"It's such a small world. My sister is retiring from the Shen Valley Community College in the valley."

"Shen Valley Community College? My aunt works there."

"Oh, come on. Really? No one has ever heard of that little school." Lewis was in disbelief. That was a remarkable coincidence.

"Would you like to ride with me?" he asked.

"We just met. I couldn't ask you that."

"Well," he said, "you're not asking. I'm offering. I'm going anyway, and while you're having the blackouts, I would not approve of you driving even if you weren't undergoing treatment."

Despite his horrible diagnosis, he still felt a little excited about a road trip with GG. "In that case," he said, "I accept. Thank you."

"You're welcome. It will be fun." He smiled that cute smile again.

Lewis blushed.

4: Mr. and Mrs. Harris

Sunday mornings at New Life Kingdom Church of Christ in Manhattan had been the same for the past 27 years. Rev. Patrick Lewis Harris, Sr., Lt. Gen. USMC Retired, finished his sermon, stepped down from the pulpit, and reached for his wife's hand.

He rarely smiled and behind his rimless eyeglasses were small, empty eyes. A man of substantial stature, he was tall with broad shoulders and somewhat still fit considering he'd retired from the USMC nearly 30 years ago. His hairline was edged perfectly and he kept what remained of his completely grey hair high and tight. His image was polished and pristine, becoming of a high-ranking military official, a general officer.

He graduated seminary just before retiring and was requested to come and lead a church where the parish felt like the congregation had spun out of control. His mission was to restore order and discipline at the NLK Church of Christ.

Mrs. Evelyn Harris, his bride of nearly 50 years, was sitting in the first seat on the front row that was commonly referred to as "The First Lady's Seat." When Rev. Harris extended his right arm toward her, she would stand, take a few steps toward him to take his hand, kiss him on the cheek, and then stand by his side, to his right side, about half a step behind him. She was to look straight ahead with dignity and poise. He would have it no other way. The live television broadcast would only portray them in the most positive light.

She was graceful and astonishingly beautiful. Her skin glowed of copper highlights and was the perfect backdrop for her wide brown eyes and gleaming bright smile. Every Sunday she had meticulously arched eyebrows, long full lashes, the right amount of blush, perfectly lined lips filled with some shade of ruby lip stain. Her hair, shoulder length and barely curled with lots of volume, always looked as if some high-profiled stylist worked his magic in a salon just moments before she arrived.

As if her beauty were not enough to envy, Mrs. Harris had style. A cosmopolitan woman, she epitomized haute couture and dressed in the highest of fashion. Her designs, not available in department stores or boutiques, were only accessible from private fashion shows held for exclusive clientele. Three times a year she'd attend the elite affairs and select her wardrobe for the season. They were tailored specifically to her frame, her comfort, and her liking. Her personal stylist accompanied her to assist with seasonal accessories. The weeklong events concluded with purchases of assembled clothes, jewelry, bags, and shoes.

On that Sunday, she was wearing a lime green Valentino, long-sleeved, knee-length dress that dropped slightly off her shoulders. She paired it with a Valentino Rockstud Leather nude pump, and, of course the matching clutch bag. Her outfit was accentuated with a tastefully lavish pair of Marci Bicego 18k gold dangling earrings. She didn't wear a necklace that day—she didn't need to because the dress draping off her shoulders gave a generous view of her gorgeous neckline and glistening collar bones. She was simply stunning.

Standing side-by-side, Rev. and Mrs. Harris had followed this ritual ever since he came to pastor the church nearly three decades ago. That small motion from them served as a queue to the congregation that it was time to extend an invitation of membership to guests who were not yet church members. If the visitors were interested in joining the church, they would stand, go down to the front, and profess their desire to officially join the NLK Church of Christ family.

One might have expected Rev. and Mrs. Harris to receive those new church members with a welcoming embrace. That was not the case. Instead, in a more dignified fashion, some appointed official would hand the new members a well-organized folder with pamphlets and information about membership at the church. All they got from Rev. Harris was a firm handshake and from Mrs. Harris, a soft smile and head nod.

She, by the way, was not allowed to speak during church services. No women were. Men of the cloth conducted orderly services, according to Rev. Harris. A woman's place was not in leadership and certainly not in speaking over men.

She stood there that Sunday thinking, I wish there could be a little spontaneity in our church and maybe more emphasis on relationship building than order. If I were allowed, I'd have a reception for new members, one without an agenda. I would plan a few hours of food and fellowship without the rigidity of a strict schedule. He'd never allow that, though. He's too chauvinistic, too conservative, and too stubborn to hear my ideas and I'm still mad about this morning. I can't believe that he ...

Rev. Harris gently squeezed her hand, ending her daydream, and prompting her to return to her seat. He had noticed that her look was different that morning. She wasn't gleaming with the blushing bride smile that the congregation and television viewers had come to expect. She looked sad or disappointed. It was not a full grimace because that would have been inappropriate and Rev. Harris certainly would not tolerate any unsuitable facial expressions from her in public, not to mention on live television.

But she was obviously different, a little distant with him and he knew the reason. She was still upset. She had been well-trained in their marriage and now, in her golden years, she'd never think of disrespecting her husband or embarrassing him. That did not mean that they wouldn't continue their discussion on the ride home.

The church service concluded with a congregational a cappella hymn. It was one of the few on the list of songs that Rev. Harris had approved. Mrs. Harris would not have called the hymns boring, but she had dreamed of instrumental accompaniment. That was another of the many sacrifices that Mrs. Harris had made for the sake of their marriage.

Mrs. Harris grew up with a pianist and organist accompanying her church choir. They even had drums, a bass guitar, and tambourines in their church. In Rev. Harris' opinion, however, they were a desecration of the service. His position was not purely biblical, but it was his view, and his alone, that dictated the order of service. They'd had that conversation many times over the years.

"Dear," she would ask him, "could we talk about a piano in church?"

"Evelyn, it is the Church of Christ policy not to allow musical instruments in church services."

"Yes, I understand that, but..."

"The policy is strictly enforced, Evelyn. If we disband one policy, then what's next? Where will it end?" He persisted, "Worldly music? Dancing? Disorder? That's what was wrong with this church. It was out of order. Before I came they were holding music concerts with those loud rowdy performances and some of those musicians were gay. Do you remember when two of them wanted to have a wedding in the church? Imagine that—a gay wedding in the House of the Lord. Do you remember how long it took me to clean up this church and restore order, Evelyn?"

Her despondency that morning was not about their ceremonial routines, his xenophobic views, his homophobia, nor his lack of respect for her opinions. There was a bigger and more pressing issue that Sunday. They had begun the discussion of their daughter's retirement party on the way to church and Mrs. Harris could hardly wait to return to their car so she could reignite that conversation.

After church, the driver, Ralph, had brought their car around front from their designated parking space. He had done so for several years and knew the routine. First, he double-checked for dust or smudges on the shiny black paint. Rev. Harris wanted the car always to shine like his shoes.

"I want to see my reflection in it," he'd say.

"Yes, Sir," Ralph responded.

Ralph, in an all black uniform, walked around the S-Class Mercedes Maybach and opened the rear right door. Rev. Harris helped Mrs. Harris into the car and closed her door. Ralph then opened the rear left door for Rev. Harris. It was done that way every time.

Mrs. Harris could wait no longer. As respectfully as possible she said to her husband, "Service was good today, Dear."

He deliberately waited a couple of minutes before responding. Finally, he replied, "You seemed bothered. I hope no one noticed. The First Lady should smile and be pleasant, always. You have an image to uphold. Don't you know your role by now?"

She dropped her head in response to his scolding, "I am sorry, Dear. I am a little bothered. Can we talk about it?"

With his voice louder and his speech more sing song, she could hear his frustration. "We have already talked, Evelyn. When Patty first called to invite us, we talked. When the invitation came in the mail, we talked. This morning on the way to church, we talked."

"Yes, and I still do not understand why we cannot go. It only takes a few hours and Ralph can drive us," she pleaded. "She's our daughter, our only daughter. I would love to see her."

He retorted, "She moved there. It was her decision. She'll be here soon for Thanksgiving."

"Yes, Dear, but we have never visited her there. Not once. In twenty years, not once. She is inviting us, her parents, to her retirement party. She wants us there to share in her joyous occasion," Mrs. Harris had not given up.

"Evelyn, you are fully aware that she defied me and chose to move there. What was she thinking? She passed up on a Wall Street career to live with bears and deer in the woods."

"She didn't want to work on Wall Street," she whispered.

"Clearly," he was becoming more aggravated and insulting, "She bought a tiny little house in the woods and took to the ways of those Indian people. She talks like them and eats like them and even dresses like them."

"I think the term is Native American, Dear, and they sound like wonderful people. They are like family to her."

"We," he said with emphasis as he waved his index finger back and forth between them, "are her family."

She spoke with a softer, childlike tone that was almost inaudible. "It was her choice, Dear. It's her life."

"Well, going this weekend would mean that we would miss our church service here on Sunday." That was the best excuse he could muster.

"You could have an associate substitute for just one Sunday. I want to visit her home, meet her friends, and experience the life that she has made for herself. We could even attend church with Patricia on Sunday."

Those were the wrong words to say to him. He yelled so loudly that it startled her and even Ralph flinched a little, "Not that church!"

"OK. Fine." She tried to calm him. "Then we can attend another church on Sunday." Her voice quivered a little as if she might be starting to cry. She had never, in 50 years of marriage, pressed for anything so desperately.

Rev. Harris was a dogged, obstinate man, but he couldn't stand to see his wife cry. "Who else will be there?" he asked.

That was encouraging because if he was asking for more details then at least he was considering taking the trip.

Mrs. Harris responded with slight excitement, "A few of Patricia's co-workers, some of her neighbors, and Ida, her best friend from college."

"What about Patrick, Jr.?"

"Yes. Lewis will attend," she continued, "and he's traveling with a friend."

Rev. Harris frowned, "Who's the friend?"

"He didn't say, but Lewis is 46 years old, never married, and has no children. I hope this friend is someone special to him. I hate the idea of him being alone."

"Do not use the word *hate* Evelyn. Please find a better way to express yourself."

"I'm sorry, Dear. It concerns me that both our children are in their 40s and still alone. I can't help but wonder if we made mistakes with them somewhere along the way."

"Not at all," he snapped. "They are both successful. He is an accountant and she is a professor."

She spoke just above a whisper, "But we don't know if they are happy. Dear, do you ever wonder if our children are happy?"

"If they're not happy, then it's their fault and not a reflection of us. We gave them the best that life has to offer. We raised them with military discipline and Christian values. We educated them and supported them through college and graduate school. They could be a little more appreciative if you asked me."

"That's true. It's just that Patricia still talks about being an athlete and Lewis never gave up on being a photojournalist."

"Those were silly ideas, Evelyn, and it's ridiculous that she's living like Little Red Riding Hood and he still plays with cameras on the weekends."

She looked out the window as she spoke, almost as if talking to herself rather than her husband, "Late 40s. Not married. No kids.

Still dreaming the same dreams of high school. Both of them. Something is missing."

Of course, Mr. Harris had an answer, "Patricia could have married, but we saved her from that running Indian. Can you imagine if we had allowed that little affair to continue what her life would be like?"

"She was in love with him, the *Iroquoian* young man. He was an Olympian. *Ned*, right? I think his name was Ned." Mrs. Harris had attempted to gently correct her husband's speech so that it would be less offensive.

"And Junior," Rev. Harris ignored her correction and kept reminiscing, "well, he's never brought a girlfriend home. Never. The only love affair he's had is with those cameras, huh?"

"Maybe he's waiting for the right person. Maybe it will be the friend he's bringing this weekend." She was hopeful.

"Evelyn," Rev. Harris had become exasperated with the conversation and wanted it to conclude, "I don't need to travel meet Junior's little friend. I don't need to stay with the bears and deer. When Patricia wants to see us or when Junior wants us to meet his new friend, they know where to find us."

Mrs. Harris could see that her husband was not going to concede and agree to the trip so she played her hold card. She didn't do this often, but when she did, it worked.

Her eyes welled full, "Dear," she said, "We are getting old. We may not have many more road trips ahead of us. What if we never have this opportunity again? I don't ask you for much. If you don't want to go, can I at least ride with Lewis so I can attend?"

Her tactics were working. It was a two-punch knockout. He couldn't stand to see her cry and he most certainly couldn't stand the thought of her going anywhere without him. He accompanied her to places where most husbands wouldn't want to go, even to her hair salon and doctors' appointments. With little hesitation he said, "Fine, Evelyn. We'll go."

"Yes, Dear. Thank you." She turned away from him, toward her window, and smiled victoriously.

5:   Ida

The morning before Patty's retirement party, she and Ida were talking on the phone.

"Good morning, Party Patty," Ida was always so bubbly. "Are you heading out for your run?"

"Yes, and I have so much to do today that I hope Rosie cooperates. I won't have time to track her down if she wanders off."

"Right. Well I'll be there to help out this afternoon. I'm packing up my car now and I'll be on the road shortly."

"Thanks, Ida." Patty sounded hurried.

"No worries. See you by lunch time."

They had bonded like sisters in college and she knew all the challenges Patty had to overcome for having the Rev. Lt. Gen. Patrick Lewis Harris, Sr., as a father. Ida was proud of how Patty had discovered her own identity and made the life that she wanted. Too bad the same couldn't be said for her mother or her brother. They all frustrated Ida.

With her Louis Vuitton luggage all packed and loaded into her silver BMW M6 convertible, she gave herself a once over in the mirror before heading out. *I've still got it,* she assured herself. Her hair had been blown out, parted in the middle, and was hanging just past her shoulders with light bouncing off the golden highlights. Her skin was still glowing from yesterday's facial and her makeup looked very natural, but took nearly an hour to apply. Her brand new C-cups bulged out of the top of her low-cut, V-neck blouse as if they were attempting to break free. Ida made sure that she was hotter in her 40s than most women in their 30s and even those in their 20s.

On the four-hour drive to her sister-friend, she had planned to make a few stops along the way. She'd have a light breakfast in Manhattan on her way out of town, pick up a package in New Jersey, and stop in D.C. for a quick visit with an old flame. That visit actually took a little longer than she had expected, but it was worth it. When she was finally back in her car, she called to check on Patty.

"Hey, Party Patty," she greeted her.

"Hey, Ida. How far along are you?"

"I'm about 45 minutes away."

"Oh, I thought you'd be closer to Shenandoah by now," Patty teased. "Got caught up in D.C. again, huh?" She laughed.

"Girl, whatever." She chuckled.

"Will you ever settle down, Ida?"

She was still driving. Although it was now November, it was still warm enough during the day to drive with her convertible top down. She adjusted her sunglasses, flipped back her hair that had blown into her face, and answered, "I will when you do."

"We'll see," Patty replied.

"You've already met him. Why won't you go for it?"

"Actually, there's recently been a development with him. I'll update you when you're get here."

Ida could hear Patty's excitement. "I can't wait to hear all the juicy details."

"They're juicy all right. I'll fill you in," she blushed and then she got that nervous feeling again. "Ida, something's not right."

Her change in tone made Ida question, "So, what's going on?"

"I don't know. It's that nervous feeling again like something is wrong."

"It could just be your nerves, Patty. You're retiring. You have a new romance. Your parents are coming for the first time since you all left Shenandoah all those years ago. Have you heard from them yet?"

"Yes, they are en route," Patty said.

"Cool. What about Lewis?"

"He and his friend have already checked into the hotel. He's not feeling well though so he's going to rest today and he'll be here at the house for the party tomorrow."

"I'm sorry he's not feeling well. I can't wait to see him and meet this new friend of his." Everyone was anxious to meet Lewis' new friend. Well, everyone except Rev. Harris.

"Me too."

"Can I pick up anything on my way? I'm on Route 66," Ida asked.

"Nothing that I can think of. I think we're good."

"OK then. I'll see you in a few minutes." Ida hung up without telling Patty that she had some dreadful feeling as well. It was almost as if some internal alarm were warning her. She shook it off as a little concern for Patty.

She wondered what the visit from Rev. Harris would entail. Would he criticize Patty or create some point of contention? It was in his combative nature. Would his compliments to Patty be insincere or laced with sarcasm? No worries though, Patty could handle him and any nitpicking or disparaging comments he might make.

Then her mind shifted to Mrs. Harris. That woman was a rare jewel. She had such a regal presence. Ida had never met anyone more dignified or poised than Mrs. Harris. Her only downfall was how beholding she'd been to her husband. Interestingly, Patty had turned out to be her antithesis. Ida wondered what Mrs. Harris would be wearing. She'd have the newest designs from the Oscar de la Renta or Versace fall collection before they hit the market.

And Lewis was in town with a friend. Ida questioned how the family would react if Lewis' friend were a man. She couldn't imagine that any of them would really be surprised. Rev. Harris would blow a gasket and overreact with some judgmental, homophobic condemnation. Mrs. Harris would take a bubble bath to escape the conflict or retreat to a corner to pray. Poor Lewis, he'd have to stand up to his father, finally. Finishing her thought as she pulled into Patty's driveway, *I'd pop a bottle and enjoy the show.*

Patty was reviewing the party plan just once more when Rosie started barking. She peeked out of a front window to see that familiar convertible coasting to a stop.

"She's here." She said to Rosie. "She's here."

Ida parked her BMW next to Patty's green 4-door Ford Explorer, threw her sunglasses onto the passenger seat, and bailed out, leaving her luggage in the car.

Rosie ran to meet her and, despite all training, rose up on her hind legs to place her front paws on Ida's legs. Ida didn't mind, not even the slight scratches on her legs from Rosie's sharp claws.

Ida greeted her, "Hey Rosie. What's up, girl?" She rubbed behind Rosie's floppy ears and looked up the walkway toward the house. She was looking for her best girl, her sister in heart.

Ida and Patty became roommates during their freshman year at NYSU. They weren't originally assigned to the same dormitory, but fate connected them. Ida's roommate smoked cigarettes. Not in the room, but the scent was in her clothes, bedding, book bag, and even her hair. Ida had gone to the campus housing office to request reassignment to another room. While she was waiting in line to fill out the change request form, she met Patty who, coincidentally, was there with the same complaint. Problem solved.

When Ida looked up from Rosie, Patty was standing out on the front porch wearing jeans and a t-shirt, holding a mug of hot tea. Her smile was as big and bright as the sun.

With only a few steps more to the front porch, Ida ran toward her. "Heyyyy," she shrieked.

Patty sat her cup down and stretched her arms toward Ida for the embrace, "Hey, Diva."

Ida said, "I'm so happy to see you."

"You look amazing," Patty complimented. "Look at you, getting younger and younger." She noticed Ida's cleavage. "So, those are your new girls? Wow."

"Yes," Ida boasted, "Nice, right? We can hook you up too."

"No thanks. I'm good, but, yes, they look great." She gestured toward Ida's car. "Let's get your things. We have so much to catch up on."

As soon as Ida stepped in the house she could smell her favorite comfort meal. "Spicy chili," she acknowledged, "and homemade rolls."

They had experimented with the recipe back in grad school and altered ingredients until they got it just right. A little more sophisticated now, they pair it with a delicious red wine.

"I hope you're hungry," Patty said.

"Yes, of course. Let's eat."

During their lunch, they began to catch up and review the final party details. Soon after they finished, Ida had a gift for Patty.

"Patty, I know I should wait until tomorrow when the other guests will have gifts as well, but I cannot wait any longer. I have something for you." Ida reached into one of her Louis Vuitton bags and retrieved a beautifully wrapped box.

"A gift, Ida? Your presence here and all your help with the party, that's gift enough."

"Yeah, whatever. Patty, you know how every morning on your run, Rosie wanders off the path to chase squirrels?" she hinted.

"Yes, of course. It's so frustrating. Sometimes her little detours take us twice as long to get home."

"Exactly. Check this out." Ida handed her the gift.

Patty opened the box and couldn't believe it. Only an incredibly talented engineer like Ida could design such a special gift.

It was a gorgeous customized bracelet with an impressive matching dog collar. Ida explained, "Just like you pair a watch or fitness bracelet with your cell phone, you pair this dog collar to the bracelet. It tracks using GPS technology. They're both made of stainless steel and will last forever." She pointed to the lettering, "What do you think of the engraving?"

"Wow. I love it, Ida. It has colorful leaves etched beautifully all the way around it. Look at the colors: red, orange, and yellow. It looks just like the design that I painted on your invitation. And my name is engraved inside, 'Patricia Harris'."

"I'm so glad you love it," Ida said.

"You designed a matching collar for Rosie?" Patty's voice was a little shaky. "Hers has her name as well, with a sunrise and a sunset imprinted on it. This is wonderful, Ida. They're perfect. How do they work? Can we try them now?"

"Of course. I've already paired and synced them."

They put the bracelet on Patty's wrist and fastened the collar onto Rosie. Then they changed into walking shoes. Patty grabbed a camera and her hiking backpack, and they headed off to walk westward toward a ravine where they could see the sunset. At first, Rosie kept up with them and did not diverge. True to form though, when they were almost there, Rosie saw squirrels. She howled and ran off after them. Patty's first instinct was to run after her but Ida reminded her that they would use the new tracking device.

"Here's how it works," Ida said pointing to the bracelet. "Press this button once and it sends a signal to her collar, similar to a dog whistle. It produces an ultra-sonic sound that will attract her to your bracelet. The signal is silent to humans, but Rosie will hear it and feel it. The vibration is gentle and will not harm her. Try it."

Patty pressed the button once and within seconds they could hear Rosie coming toward them. Her paws were moving quickly through the rustling leaves. It was working. Rosie was running toward the signal from Patty's bracelet.

"Try this," Ida continued. "Here's the really cool part. Press and hold this other button and speak. If she's within 20 feet, she can also hear your voice through the speaker on her collar."

Patty called out to Rosie through the microphone on her bracelet and Rosie barked in response. She was amazed. "It's perfect, Ida."

"I'm glad you love it. There's one more feature. It is charged with solar energy. When you come out for your morning run, both your bracelet and her collar will charge automatically. No need to buy batteries. Also, they're stainless steel and weather resistant so you don't have to take them off often."

"Got it, and my bracelet is so beautiful that it looks like fine jewelry. I can't believe you put my artwork on it. I won't want to take it off. How long does the charge last?"

"About 48 hours."

"Thank you, Ida. You're the best. This is awesome. Thank you so much. You must have worked on this for a very long time."

"You're welcome, my friend. I'm glad you like it."

The three of them were approaching Patty's house when they saw a car parking next to Ida's. Rosie took off ahead of them to greet the guests.

6: Back to Campus

Ida and Patty were coming back from their walk when Rosie ran up to a car that had a U-Haul attached. A few of the college's music students were delivering the piano.

"We're sorry we're a little late, Miss Harris. We had to leave the wine festival, pick up the U-Haul, and then find Mr. Ned to unlock the music room," one of them explained.

"Oh, I was aware. This is fine," Patty replied. "I really appreciate it."

They unloaded the baby grand piano and its bench and carried them into her living room. She had made space for it in the far corner and draped a cover over it that she would remove after dinner. Just as they walked out, she ran behind to them ask for her sheet music.

"I thought I left it with the piano when I practiced yesterday," she told them.

"We didn't see it, Miss Harris," they responded. "We're very sorry."

She checked her watch. It was still early. "Well, they're not here. I must have left them in my desk. I'll run over to pick them up."

"We would go for you but we have to get back to the festival, Miss Harris," the other one said sincerely.

"No worries," she said. "I have time to get them. Thanks for delivering the piano, guys. Enjoy the festival."

When they left, she looked to Ida and said, "It looks like I have to run over to campus quickly. I'll be right back."

"I'll come with you."

"Thanks, but I really could use you here. We have so much to do to prepare the food for tomorrow."

"OK, well I'll get started in the kitchen." Then Ida looked down at Rosie and said, "I hope you'll keep me company, girl," as she grabbed a wine bottle and her glass and moved toward the kitchen.

"Rosie will be great company for you. I'll be back in about half an hour," Patty told her as she grabbed her keys and purse, wrapped her shawl around her neck, and moved quickly to her truck.

As she was driving to campus and recalling what the students had just told her, that the doors were locked when they were there, she was afraid she wouldn't be able to get into the building. She called Ned from Campus Security.

"Hey, Babe," he answered his phone.

"Hi, Sweetie. I need a favor."

"Sure. What's up?"

"I think I left my sheet music in my classroom. I'm heading to campus to pick it up. Are the doors locked?"

"Yes, all but one. I left the door closest to the music room unlocked so they could get the piano for you. I'm helping out at the wine festival and won't be back to lock it for another few hours. You can use that entrance."

"Thanks so much."

"No problem, Babe. Just let me know if you need anything else," he said so sweetly.

"I'm sorry again about my party, Honey. My parents…"

He interrupted, "Patty, you don't have to explain yourself. We've had this conversation. All that matters is that we are together again. Your father will not come between us this time, OK?"

"You're right and we'll have the rest of our lives to celebrate."

"We sure will. Drive safely. Call me if you need anything."

"I will. I love you."

"And I love you." When that call ended, Patty was thinking of how relieved she would be to tell everyone their news.

She arrived at campus to the odd-shaped, two-story building. An Iroquoian family had donated the land for the school and its shape was unique—similar to an isosceles triangle. The architect designed a building to maximize the lot.

The location was in the center of the valley, surrounded by mountain views. All of the classes, along all three sides of the building, had huge windows making all the sights visible from within the building.

The shortest side was the front of the building. The two sides of equal length comprised the east and west wings. The center of the triangle was a courtyard. Students would often hang out there or use it as a shortcut between the administration wing and the east wing and west wing.

Patty noticed that all the lights were off. It was obvious that no one else was there. The front wing, where she entered the faculty and staff parking lot, housed all of the administrative offices. The west wing had all of the business, technology, and law classes. Patty's classroom was in the middle of that wing, on the second floor. The east wing is where the liberal arts classes were, including the music room on the first floor. During regular school hours, she could park on the east wing and walk upstairs to her classroom. Not today.

Because the only unlocked door was on the east wing, she drove around to that entrance. She had to navigate the long hallways to the other side of the building and then go upstairs to her classroom. All other doors were locked, so she couldn't even cut across the courtyard, but all was not lost. She still had on her sneakers from her earlier outing with Ida and Rosie and thought that in an empty building she could sprint to her classroom. It would be fun.

Before entering the building, she sent a few text messages. She realized that she hadn't spoken with her parents or her brother all afternoon, so she reached out to them. She wanted Estelle to know that she could head over to Patty's house to help Ida with food preparation and the floral arrangements, so she sent Estelle a message as well. Patty hoped that by the time she dashed in and out of the building, they would have responded.

She dropped her cell phone into her purse and was getting out of her car when it occurred to her that she could sprint faster without her bag and wrap. She put them in the passenger seat and locked the doors. With her keys tucked into her pockets, her hands were free for a great sprint.

She flipped the light switch on in the music room and looked around the piano area, but, just as the guys had said, her sheet music was not there. She had to look in her classroom. The lights were off in the hallways, but the daylight still peered through windows and the skylights enough to allow her to meander the corridors.

Thinking that it might be darker by the time she returned, she turned back to leave the lights on in the music room. Just as she was leaving the music room the second time, the building began to shake. It was not a violent shaking and did not toss her around or destroy any property, but it was enough to startle her. *Could this be an earthquake?* she thought. She had never experienced one, so she wasn't sure.

Thankfully, it only lasted for a few seconds. Once the shaking stopped, she sprinted, running as fast as she could to her classroom. She ran down the hallway on the first floor toward the vertex, where the east and west wings connected. After turning that corner, she ran up the stairs and was in her classroom in a matter of seconds. That run reminded her of her days of indoor track.

Her sheet music was on her desk. She picked it up and then noticed that she was standing in the very spot where she prayed every morning before class started. The shaking started again. That time it was more rapid and her first thought was about the closest exit. All the doors were locked on that wing of the building. Her heart began pounding and she knew that if another, and more severe episode, occurred, she could be trapped in the building or worse, if the building—made mostly of glass—collapsed. She wished she'd had her cell phone with her, but it was in her truck.

She decided to go for it and began to sprint back toward the east wing when the shaking began again. Unfortunately, it was much worse that time.

7:   The Hotel

Lewis and GG were relaxing in their suite, perusing the schedule for the wine festival to determine where GG's favorites were in the lineup, when the shaking began. Lewis jumped up to secure his photography equipment.

He had unpacked lights and lenses and he was charging batteries. They were fully charged when he left home, but the ride down the east coast was so scenic that he had GG make several stops along the way so he could take pictures. Because of the fatigue, he had to take many of the photos from the passenger seat of GG's car with the window down. For a few of the shots, GG helped Lewis move to the back of his Range Rover. With the hatch up, Lewis could take pictures from the tailgate.

Lewis was enjoying himself until he thought about spending a weekend in the presence of his father. That thought made him, habitually, reach for a cigar. GG was not surprised.

"What do you escape?"

Lewis didn't understand. "What do you mean?"

"Your eyes drifted to a far away place, your demeanor changed, and then you reached for a cigar. I'm not judging. I'm just curious. What did you see?"

"My dad."

Sensing Lewis' discomfort with the conversation, GG changed the subject. "It's beautiful here."

"Yes. My sister loves her life here." Holding his camera up, "I can't wait to show her these pictures."

He was excited to see her and prayed that he'd have the strength to photograph her party. The initial treatments were helping the cough, but draining his energy. They hadn't really helped with the blackouts so, thanks to GG, he had made it safely to town.

During the second shaking episode, GG was on the phone with his Auntie E. She wasn't his biological aunt, but was a dear friend to his mother and she was very active in rearing GG and Harry. She and GG had an even more special relationship because she seemed to be comfortable with his identity while the rest of the family was not. He appreciated her.

"Hello, Auntie E. This is GG," he said on the phone.

"Hi, Baby. Are you in town yet?"

"Yes, Ma'am," he said, "and I brought a friend with me."

"Great, Baby," she squealed, "I can't wait to meet him."

Interesting, he thought, *I didn't say that it was a 'him.'* "Thanks, Auntie E. We have plans for dinner this evening, but how about we stop by afterward?"

"Perfect, GG. I have dinner plans, also, so I'll see you later this evening."

"Sure. Love you, Auntie E!"

"Love you too, Baby. Bye-bye."

GG went into the other room of their suite to check on Lewis, who was sound asleep. He checked Lewis' pulse; it was a little slow, but not alarming. He also checked the schedule for Lewis' next medication dose and noted that it was not yet time. He retired to the sofa to relax and the building shook. He turned the TV channel to the local news to see if anything were being reported. The building shook again—this time more forcefully. Nothing was being reported on the news, so he called the hotel front desk. No one answered.

"Fine," he said aloud. "I'll just go down there." He checked on Lewis once more and then headed down to the hotel lobby.

When he entered the elevator, an over-the-top couple was inside and obviously annoyed that they had to stop on his floor. The husband spoke in one-word statements.

"Hello," he said.

"Hi. How are you all?" GG greeted them.

"Well," the woman replied. The man said nothing.

"Did you feel that shaking?" GG asked them.

"Naturally," the husband muttered.

GG looked them over and couldn't help but think of the movie, *Coming to America*. That couple in their overstated designer clothing and extravagant luggage, lots of it, reminded him of King Jaffe Joffer and his Queen of Zamunda. He couldn't help but ask the obviously misplaced couple, "Are you here for your son, Prince Akeem?" and he began to laugh at his own joke.

Having no knowledge of what GG was asking, the husband replied, "Pardon?"

Before GG could reply, the building began to shake again. The husband pushed his wife into a rear corner of the elevator and stood in front of her. His feet were spread apart and he stretched himself to hold onto the guardrails. With his left hand on one rail and his right hand on the other, he stood tall and strong and assured her that she'd be OK. She answered him with a barely perceptible whisper, "Thank you, Dear." Her arms were wrapped around his waist and she held on to him tightly. Their wheeled luggage began to roll around the elevator.

The elevator stopped between floors. The lights went out. The air shut off. They had lost power.

The husband belted in frustration, "Seriously!"

GG said, "We've lost power."

"Really, Sherlock?" belted the belligerent husband.

"We must have power." GG began, "My friend is sick and …."

The husband interrupted, "Quiet!"

"Excuse me. Who are you?" GG was losing his patience.

"We must strategize," said the husband.

"My friend is sick and …," GG attempted again, but was interrupted.

"Not now, Little Man," warned the husband.

Just then the elevator buttons illuminated indicating that the hotel's backup generator was working. GG pushed the button for the floor above, sending the elevator back up.

"What are you doing?" asked the husband. "We must vacate this God-forsaken building immediately."

GG took a couple of deep breaths. Just as the elevator door opened on his floor, he moved their luggage out of his way. He had considered picking up pieces and tossing them, but with enough self-control he was actually gentle with them. He stepped out and then looked back to the couple. "My friend upstairs is very ill and his medical equipment requires electricity." Then, as the doors were closing, he concluded, "he could die, you pompous son-of-a-bitch!"

GG ran down the hall to their suite and swiped his key card, but it didn't work. He knocked several times on the door, but Lewis never answered. The power outage or the building shaking must have affected the room key cards, he thought. He'd have to head down to the front desk again. This time, reluctant to use the elevators, he entered the stairwell and ran down several flights to the main floor.

He burst through the door from the stairs into the lobby and many guests had congregated in the lobby with questions. GG asked a gentleman near the back of the crowd what was going on. The man explained that they were all concerned about the shaking and electricity and that a man had bulldozed his way to the front and was demanding answers. GG stretched to see ahead. The couple from the elevator was at the front desk and the husband was speaking with the hotel manager.

He could hear the husband, "This is unsatisfactory. We are checking out immediately and will be sure to contact your corporate offices about our experience." Holding his wife by the hand, he cleared a path to the front door.

GG could see out the front door that their car and driver awaited them. A gentleman in a black uniform had loaded their luggage and walked around the S-Class Mercedes Maybach and opened the rear right door for the husband to help his wife into the car. GG shook his head and tried to figure out a way to get answers to his many questions.

After several minutes, when he finally approached the service desk, he asked about his key card. The lights flickered. Then he wanted to know how long they could rely on generator power. The manager was not sure. They were waiting to hear back from their building engineer.

GG, thinking quickly, called Auntie E back.

"Hi Auntie. Quick question. There was a shaking and then the hotel power went out. We are on generator power, but we're not sure how long that will last. Have you lost power, Auntie E?"

"No, Baby, I haven't. I felt the shaking too, but my power is fine."

"Auntie E, my friend's medical equipment must have electricity. I hate to ask but…"

She cut him off, "Sure, Baby. You and your friend can stay here. I'm going out to help a friend with dinner, but I'll leave the key in the usual place. If you get here before I return just let yourself in and make yourself at home."

"Thank you, Auntie E. We really appreciate it."

"No probably, GG. I'm glad to have you stay at the house. See you soon."

He ended the call and began to navigate through the crowd to the stairwell entrance. He needed to get up to the suite to check on Lewis quickly.

When he entered the room, Lewis was awake. "Hi, there," he said.

"Hi, Lewis. How are you feeling?"

"Not bad," he answered.

GG ran over to check his machines and seemed stressed. "Are you OK?" Lewis asked him.

"Fine. Did the shaking or power outage bother you?"

"Huh? What shaking? What outage?" Lewis had no idea what had happened.

"The building shook a few times and then the power went out," GG explained. The hotel is temporarily on generator power, but we don't know how long that will last. My Auntie E says her electricity is fine that we can stay with her, so I'll gather our things."

"Is that necessary?" Lewis asked. "Won't we be fine here?"

"I'm not taking that risk, Lewis. We are checking out and staying with my Auntie E."

Seeing that GG's mind was made up, Lewis agreed. He attempted to stand, but did not have balance and toppled over. GG caught him before he hit the floor.

"Lewis, you're too weak to walk. We have to use the wheelchair."

If he'd had enough energy to put up a fight he would have, but under the circumstances, and he agreed with GG.

GG helped Lewis into the wheelchair and had him wait in the room while he made several trips downstairs to load their belongings into his car. On his final trip down, he asked the hotel manager if someone could assist him with transporting Lewis. They asked why he couldn't use the elevator and explained that the one elevator experience was all he could endure for that day.

Once in the car, they were ready to head over to Patty's for a quick visit before settling in at Auntie E's house for the evening.

8:   At Patty's House

Ida was in Patty's kitchen arranging hors d'oeuvres for that evening. They had agreed that after the family had traveled such a long distance for the party, and given the history of dissension, that they would prepare a nice dinner for them. Their intention was to make amends before the party the following day.

Patty had been both excited and nervous. Ida marveled at how organized all the food and drinks were in the kitchen. Lots of effort had gone into making that evening's dinner and the party on the following day special.

Just as Ida was about to slide a tray of miniature crab cakes into the oven, Rosie came to her and stood up on her hind feet. She stood there for a few seconds then retrieved her leash in her mouth and sat by the front door. Ida responded, "Good girl, Rosie. You obviously need to go out." She opened the door, motioned outward, and said, "Go." Rosie ran to a tree and Ida decided to leave her out there for a few minutes while she continued to warm the appetizers.

The house shook a little.

"Whoa," Ida said. "What's that?"

A few seconds later, it shook again but worse. "What the hell? An earthquake? Here? Now?"

The lights flickered a few times and then the power went out. "OK then." She called Patty to ask where she kept the flashlights, but there was no answer. Thinking quickly, she used the flashlight on her phone to look through cabinets and drawers, but couldn't find one. Finally, she remembered that Patty used her attic for storage.

She'd have to go up there, so she turned the oven off just in case the power came back on while she was in another room. She wouldn't want to ruin the dinner.

Holding the half-full wine bottle in one hand and her phone in the other, she made her way to the hallway where the cord dropped for the attic stairs. Holding both, she managed to climb up into the ceiling.

She checked her phone again, but Patty still had not called her back. Patty was only supposed to be gone for 30 minutes, but more time had passed. Then there was the mini earthquake experience and now the lights were out. She sent a text message to check on Patty and was afraid that Patty's dinner wouldn't go well, but it was still too early to panic.

Not surprisingly, the attic was more organized than most people's homes. It could've easily been a consignment shop or vintage store. Christmas decorations and ornaments were labeled in green bins with matching lids. Trophies, tons of the them, were arranged in cabinets, chronologically. Seasonal clothes and shoes were in marked boxes.

There was a container for Storm Supplies. "My girl," Ida yelled and held up the wine bottle to the container as if toasting Patty. She turned on a battery-powered lantern and had a much better view of the room. Over in a corner there was a chest that was not labeled. It was intriguing.

Ida was curious why it looked different from all the other boxes and bins. It was an older chest and it was isolated from the other boxes. She thought briefly that opening it, especially after finding what she had come up there for, would be an invasion of Patty's privacy. Snooping. "Yeah," she said, "I wanna know."

There were diaries, volumes of them, and the earliest dated back to middle school. Ida knew that Patty had kept diaries when they were younger, but assumed they had all been discarded long ago. She had certainly burned her own for fear that someone could someday read them. Patty had, on the other hand, kept a new log every year and they were in mint condition.

They might have made an interesting read, but Ida was more curious to see what else was in the special trunk. There was a copy of her Last Will and Testament in a sealed envelope. There were also letters to her parents, her brother, and Ida, in the event that something happened to her. That caused anxiety for Ida and she prayed that they would not need those letters for a long time.

There was also a very old shoebox labeled, "From Grandpa." It only contained a Bible. According to the postage, he had mailed it to Patty when she moved to the Valley 20 years ago. It contained recordings of their family genealogy dated back to the 1920s. Every few decades, the handwriting would change, indicating the continuation of the tradition. It chronicled names and birthdays with branches down to each generation. Ida read off the names to see if it were Patty's paternal or maternal lineage. None of the names were familiar. How odd that it did not list either Rev. or Mrs. Harris. There was also no mention of Patty or Lewis. The last recordings were in the 1940s, when her parents should have been listed. Ida turned the page to see what followed and, interestingly, the next page had been torn out.

"All right," she said. "There are secrets and they must be big ones to have removed them from this Bible. I wonder if Patty knows what they are."

The lights came back on. Ida didn't want to bring the Bible down from the chest, but she was interested in researching the family tree. She took a picture of the chronicle with her cell phone and returned all the contents back to the chest just as she had found them. She brought the lantern with her in case the lights went out again and descended the wobbly stairs.

She then texted Lewis.

"Hey. Have you heard from Patty?"

"No. Why? Everything OK?"

"I'm sure it is, but she left to run a quick errand and I thought she'd be back by now."

"Nope. Nothing. We are on our way to her house though. Should be there shortly."

"We?"

"Yes, my friend is driving. I'm a little under the weather."

"I see," then she had a thought, "Hey. I could use a favor."

"Sure. What's up?"

"I found pages in her Bible that I think represent your family tree. It would be cool to see photos of your ancestors. What do you think?"

"Great idea. I like it. I have subscriptions to genealogy websites and registers so it wouldn't take me long to trace our lineage."

"OK, I'm sending you a photo of the log. Oh, and one more thing, it ends in the 1940s. I wonder if you can complete it to date."

"I'll certainly try," he said.

"Cool. See you soon."

Ida went back into the kitchen to resume with the food preparation and then realized that Rosie hadn't come back to the door yet.

"You've got to be kidding me!" she thought. "Now I have to go look for Rosie. I'd better do it now because it will be dark soon."

She checked her phone once more and still nothing from Patty. Dinner would not be ready by the time the family arrived and now she had to go out into the woods at dusk searching for the dog.

"Rosie! Rosie! Here, girl."

Nothing. She recalled how frustrated Patty would become when describing Rosie's wanderings and with that same annoyance, sang her name, "Rooooooooosie." Still nothing.

She made her way up to the path they had walked earlier. The sun was beginning to set as she reached the top. Looking down into the valley she couldn't believe what she saw. Mass amounts of the earth had shifted. Buildings had collapsed. Some regions were still in the dark. She realized then that there had in fact been an earthquake.

Her heart began to race. "Oh my God! Patty! Oh my God! Where's Patty?" She headed back down to the house hoping that Lewis and his friend had arrived. There was no time to look for Rosie. She had to find Patty first.

She tried calling Patty again, but there was no answer. She called Lewis.

"Where are you?" she asked.

"We are pulling into the driveway. What's wrong?"

"Lewis, there was an earthquake. Did you feel it?"

"No," he answered. "I think I slept through it. Are you OK, Ida?"

"No, no, I'm fine. Patty is missing. She left before the earthquake and should have been back by now, but I haven't heard back from her. I can't reach her."

"We're parking now."

"I'll be right there. I had to go look for Rosie. She's also missing. I'm walking back toward the house."

As she approached the house, she could see their car lights. A rather handsome gentleman had unfolded a wheelchair and was taking it around to the passenger door of a white Range Rover.

Ida yelled, "Hello!"

The gentleman responded, "Hi. I'm GG." He gestured toward the passenger seat and said, "Lewis is here."

Ida walked around to that side of the car and was perplexed at what she saw. Lewis had lost weight and did not look well. His eyes were sunken and he was frail. GG was helping him into a wheelchair and he was connected to an oxygen tank and tubes and machines.

"Lewis?" Her eyes welled with tears and she bent down to hug him. "Hi, Honey. It's getting chilly out here. Let's get you inside."

"Hi, Ida. Good to see you." His voice was weak. His speech was slow. His breathing was labored. "Patty?" was all he could muster up enough energy to ask.

"Not yet," she answered.

Ida and GG were able to get Lewis inside where he could sit comfortably by the fire. That would help with the chills and shivering. GG plugged in all of the equipment that required electricity, draped a blanket around Lewis' shoulders, and administered medication.

Ida offered to help, but GG had it all covered. "Hot tea, please?" he asked. "I think he might enjoy something warm to drink."

"Sure. Coming right up." She turned toward the kitchen and then thought she heard another car outside.

"Patty!" She ran to the front porch. There was in fact a car, but not Patty's car. It was the Mercedes—the Harrises' Mercedes.

She didn't walk out to the car to greet them. She didn't even wait out on the porch. Instead, she turned and went back inside.

"Patty?" Lewis asked her.

"No," she shook her head. "Your parents," she said between gritted teeth. After a heavy sigh, she repeated, "Your parents."

Deciding that she just wasn't in the mood to cook, she returned to the kitchen to turn everything off. They'd figure out food later. The driver entered the house before Rev. and Mrs. Harris. He inquired as to the quarters where he should place their luggage. Ida thought they were staying at the hotel so she was confused and asked Ralph, "what's all this?"

"The power is out at their hotel. All the others are full because of the wine festival. Rev. and Mrs. Harris will be lodging here, Ma'am."

"Where will you stay, Ralph?"

"I will be returning to the hotel. The power outage doesn't really bother me," he explained.

Ida pointed toward the hallway and said simply, "OK then. In a room, please." She watched him bring a full set, at least eight pieces of matching bags, down the hall. Digressing slightly, she admired the craftsmanship and was curious as to the designer of such impressive luggage. *"Gorgeous bags!"* she murmured. Her thoughts were abruptly interrupted when the Harrises entered the room.

"Rev. and Mrs. Harris," she had begun to greet them when she heard a car door close outside. "Patty!" she hoped.

She brushed past the Harrises and ran to the front porch. Another car, yes, but not Patty. A lady, possibly Estelle, was walking briskly toward the front door. Ida peered from left to right, scanning the woods quickly for Rosie while waiting for the lady visitor, but still no sign of her.

9:   Family

Lewis was still having chills and GG went into the kitchen to check on the tea. The Harrises had entered the living room where Lewis sat slouched over in a wheelchair, but had not recognized him. He was drifting in and out of consciousness and was not yet aware that they were in the room.

Ida was outside greeting the hurried lady who was stepping up onto the porch. "Hello," Ida said. "I'm Ida, Patty's friend."

Estelle looked up at her, "Hey, Ida. It's me, Estelle. Nice to see you."

"Oh, Estelle. Hello! Come on in."

"Is Patty here?"

"No, Ma'am. She's not. I've been trying to reach her."

As Estelle entered, GG came from the kitchen and was surprised, "Auntie E, what are you doing here?"

Estelle was shocked as well, "GG, Baby, what you are doing here?"

Lewis heard their exchange and asked in amazement, "You two know each other?"

When Rev. and Mrs. Harris heard Lewis speak they recognized his voice. "Lewis!" they shouted in astonishment.

GG saw the Harrises and exclaimed, "King Joffer!" He then looked at Lewis and said, "that makes you Prince Akeem!"

Ida burst into laughter and uncorked another wine bottle.

Mrs. Harris instinctively moved toward Lewis with open arms, wanting to hug him when Mr. Harris stopped her. "No dear. He's sick. Look at him."

"Sick, yes. Contagious, no." GG retorted. "His condition is not communicable, not transmissible."

Not offering any wine to others, Ida filled her glass to the rim. Holding it in one hand, she stretched out her other arm with her fingers spread wide and lowered it dramatically as if pressing something down slowly. She said, "let's all sit down, calm down, and sort this out."

Everyone took a seat. GG had pulled a dining room chair over near Lewis by the fireplace. Ida and Estelle sat on the love seat on the far wall. Rev. and Mrs. Harris were on the sofa, but sat so closely together that it left plenty of room for others.

After two big gulps of the wine and a few moments of silence, Ida began to speak. "I will make the introductions that are obviously in order, but, first and foremost, has anyone heard from Patty?"

"What do you mean?" asked Mrs. Harris. Isn't she here?"

GG shook his head in disbelief. "*Could this woman be more dense?*" he muttered under his breath.

"No, Ma'am," Ida responded. She left to run an errand and said that she'd return quickly. She texted me once but I haven't heard from her since and it's been a couple of hours. I've called and left messages, but she's not responding. When I went out to look for Rosie, who has apparently run off, I noticed power outages and some structural damage, so I'm very concerned."

"The earthquake knocked out power grids," Estelle explained. "She texted me a couple of hours ago as well." She then looked at GG, still perplexed.

"Baby, what are you doing here?"

"Auntie E, this is my friend that I was telling you about. His name is Lewis."

Greeting the feeble man in the wheelchair, "We've met before, Lewis. It's been a while and it's very nice to see you," she said. "Patty's brother, right? and…"

She was abruptly interrupted by Rev. Harris. "If the reunion is over now, please excuse us." He stood and reached for his wife's hand. "We are leaving. Ralph will retrieve our belongings."

With incredulity, Ida, GG, and Estelle all stood and began to speak at the same time. "Rev. Harris…"

He stunned them when he shouted, "Silence!" He then fastened the single button on his sports coat, took a deep breath to compose himself, and retorted, "We have traveled all this way to this God-forsaken place. The long ride was arduous. The hotel was substandard to say the least. Patty doesn't have the decency to meet us here at her home. Our son obviously has that despicable disease that I imagine he contracted from his little friend here." And then he pointed to Ida and continued, "and D-Cup, the alcoholic, is in charge. We are out of here."

Just then there was a knock at the door. All of the houseguests looked toward the door, but none moved. After a moment, Estelle dashed across the room and greeted the newest visitor.

"Ned?"

"Hi, Ms. Estelle. Is Patricia here?"

"No, she isn't, honey. We're very concerned," she said. "Patty is missing. Please come in. Her family is here."

Estelle introduced Ned. "Everyone, this is Ned, our Campus Security Manager."

"You've got to be kidding me," barked Rev. Harris. "The little running Indian boy?"

They all ignored him.

Estelle continued, "Ned, these are Patty's parents, Rev. and Mrs. Harris; her brother Lewis and his friend, GG, who's also my nephew; and her best friend, Ida."

"Pleased to meet you all. Has anyone heard from Patricia?"

They all shook their heads.

"OK, when was the last time anyone had communication with her?" Lewis and Ida began to review their calls log and text messages. She had texted Ida, Lewis, and Estelle when she arrived on campus. She had left a voicemail on Mrs. Harris' phone.

She had made the one call to Ned. He explained, "She called me about gaining access to the building a couple of hours ago. I couldn't call to check on her because the quake affected our cell towers. Not being able to call and check on her, I thought I'd come by. She should have been home by now."

Rev. Harris had become remarkably concerned, "Access to what building? Where? When?"

Ida and Ned spoke at the same time. "Patricia had left sheet music in the school and ran over to retrieve them. She thought they might be in the music room or her classroom."

"Why would she need sheet music?" Rev. Harris was baffled.

Estelle answered, "She plays piano. We were going to surprise you with a duet this evening."

Mrs. Harris burst into tears. "Patricia? My Patricia? She plays piano?"

"Yes. She's classically trained. She borrowed the piano there in the corner from the school for this evening."

"Right," Ida interjected. She was nervous, speaking even faster than normal. "When they delivered the piano, her sheet music was missing, so she drove back over to the school to get it. I've been calling and texting, but she's not responding."

Ned announced, "I'm going to the school."

"I'm coming with you," said Rev. Harris. "Me too," they each began to chime in.

"No." Rev. Harris answered. "We don't know what to expect at the school. There are power outages, warped roads, and collapsed buildings. We also need a base to check back in with updates."

Lewis spoke up. "I'm coming, too."

GG cautioned him, "That's not a good idea, Lewis. Why don't we stay here while they go?"

"I agree with your friend, Lewis," Mrs. Harris whispered. "Your equipment needs to be plugged in for electricity."

"No, it doesn't, Mom. It has a battery backup," he explained.

GG confirmed, "Yes, the battery backup lasts for up to 12 hours, but I still don't think it's a good idea."

Just when she heard *battery backup*, Ida had a recollection. "Wait! Wait! Um, Rosie."

Rev. Harris, as if on cue, rudely interrupted again, "We are not concerned about the dog right now. We are going to find Patricia."

"Exactly," Ida continued. "Rosie is wearing a collar that has a GPS tracking device installed. Patty is wearing the bracelet that is paired to the collar. If Patty cannot use her cell phone, she can use the bracelet to signal her location to Rosie. It also has a camera and microphone. She can communicate with us."

"That's brilliant," Ned said.

"Thank you, Ned. I designed and made them as a gift for Patty's retirement. Not bad, huh?" and she turned to Rev. Harris in sarcasm, "for D-cups and wine."

"That will help. Where's Rosie?" he asked.

"She ran off earlier. I think during the power outage. I was out looking for her when Lewis arrived."

Rev. Harris took charge. "Listen up. Ned and I will go over to the school. Ned, we'll need flashlights and shovels. If your security office has walkie-talkies or something that will allow us to communicate, we should get them also. Ropes, chains, knives, a compass, and any other rescue gear you have."

"Yes, Sir," Ned answered. "I should have most of that in my truck outside. I'll go check."

Rev. Harris then turned to GG and continued, "You and Ida go find Rosie. Stay together. When you find her, bring her to the school to wherever Ned's truck is parked. If you cannot reach us via cell phone, hit the horn on your truck when you arrive. We will know to come to you. Do not come to look for us. Park by his truck and wait. Do you follow?"

"Yes, Sir," GG replied and with a hint of admiration of this arrogant, ostentatious being who had transformed into a calm, focused commander.

GG then looked at Lewis, "When we find Rosie, we'll come back by here and pick you up on the way to the school. We will not go there without you."

Lewis looked relieved, "Thank you."

Rev. Harris then addressed Estelle and Mrs. Harris. "You two stay here, man the base, and use Patricia's land line to make calls. Try to contact Ralph and send him to the school. Reach out to the Coast Guard, Red Cross, and local authorities. Send anyone who can get into this valley to the community college to assist with a rescue mission. The power may go out again, so get bottled water, gather flashlights, prepare the foods that might spoil. Stay here, together."

"Yes, Dear," Mrs. Harris answered him, "and please be careful."

GG checked on Lewis ensuring that his equipment was plugged in and he was comfortable. He helped him from the wheelchair to the sofa and asked Mrs. Harris if she could get snacks for him. It was time for another medical treatment, but he had tolerated it better with food. Knowing that he needed to leave immediately to help find Rosie, he gave Estelle and Mrs. Harris instructions for caring for Lewis. He and Ida headed off into the woods.

Rev. Harris met Ned out at the back of his truck where he was taking inventory of equipment. There were ample rescue supplies. With Ned driving and Rev. Harris in the passenger seat, they were headed off toward the college.

Mrs. Harris was in the kitchen making snacks for Lewis and planning to cook. She was impressed with how many preparations had been made and stopped very briefly to take in the decorations and organization of her daughter's kitchen.

Estelle had added more wood to the fireplace and was in the living room mixing the cocktail for Lewis's intravenous drip. Her nephew had given her specific instructions and she was confident that she could do this for Lewis. She desperately wanted to ask how they'd met and come to know one another, but the timing seemed inappropriate for inquiring. *And this poor baby,* she thought, *is so sick. God help him.*

10: Danger

Ida and GG were hiking uphill in search for Rosie when they began to make small talk. Both were nervous and grateful for the other's company.

"So," he began, "you're Patty's friend? How long have you two been together?"

"Together? We're not together. We are best friends."

"Oh, I'm sorry" he said. "I didn't know."

"No, it's OK." She didn't want to insult him. "It's OK for same sex to be together. You know, I mean, I'm not homophobic." She wanted to stop, but couldn't and wondered if it were her nerves or the wine that had her stumbling over her words and rambling.

He chuckled, "Neither am I. My apologies if I made you uncomfortable. Let's start again."

"OK," she exhaled, appreciative of his understanding.

"My name is Gary Goldstein. Most people call me GG. Lewis and I are just recently acquainted."

She smiled and returned the pleasantry. "My name is Ida. Patty and I have been best friends since college. I came to town to help her with her retirement party."

"To town? From where?" he asked her.

"New York."

"Me too. I come to visit my Auntie E as often as I can."

She was curious. "How is Ms. Estelle your aunt?"

"Well," he searched for words, "it's really interesting. I have a twin named Harry. Our parents died in a car accident when our mother was expecting us. Auntie E and our mother were very good friends. She was riding with them on their way to our baby shower when they were hit head on by a drunk driver.

By the time the paramedics arrived on the scene, my mother had gone into labor. Auntie E delivered both my brother and me. She actually had a brief conversation with our mother before her passing. She promised that she would always be in our lives and look after us. Even after our biological aunt and uncle adopted us and moved us to New York, Auntie E kept in touch."

"I'm so sorry for your loss," Ida said. "Estelle was a God-send to you. Patty has wonderful stories about her."

"Yes, I imagine so. When we were children, our favorite times were in the summer with Auntie E."

Ida was calling out for Rosie again and GG joined her. There was still no answer. They continued to hike and converse, "What do you do in New York?"

"I'm an engineer at an electronics R&D firm. Basically, I build prototypes for innovative tech gadgets."

"Ah, that explains the dog collar. One of your designs, I presume?"

"Yes. I was trying to solve Patty's problem of Rosie running off, getting lost, and then, with her hearing weakening, being a real challenge to find. Yet, here we are, in the woods in the dark, looking for her. Ironic, huh?"

They continued to call out for Rosie as they waved their flashlights around. They could hear the sounds of various birds, rustling leaves, and, far off in the distance, sirens. The rescue squads must have been busy.

It was a clear evening and they could see the full moon through the treetops. The temperature had dropped and the sun had set so it was dark and a little chilly out.

"Dear God," she said aloud, "please let Patty be OK." Her voice trembled.

"Amen," GG finished. He then changed the subject to take her mind off of Patty, the cool air, and the bleakness of the entire situation for a while. "Best friends since college, so you must know the Harris family pretty well."

"Yes, I do. They're like family to me, kind of."

"Kind of?" he asked.

"Patty and I are very close. She's the sister I never had. Lewis is the brother I never had. The parents, well, I have parents."

"I see," he said. I met the parents earlier in the hotel when the power went out. They are quite the couple."

"Yes, to put it kindly. How do you know Lewis?"

"We met at a wedding," he answered. "Well, at several weddings."

"Oh, sounds romantic. Tell me about it," she pried.

"He photographs our family's events. Recently, he was photographing my niece's wedding and I mustered the courage to speak to him." He began to tell Ida the whole story and shared some details, but—protecting Lewis' privacy—he did not discuss his diagnosis.

Of course, Ida could see from Lewis' physical condition and detect in the soberness of GG's tone, that the prognosis was not good. "Well," she responded, "I'm glad that he has you in his life, especially now." While GG did not need her approval, he was grateful for her blessing.

"We should keep in touch once we're back in New York," he told her.

"I'd like that," and then she thought she heard something. "Do you hear that? What is that sound?"

GG heard it as well. "Whimpering." They beckoned for Rosie more frantically and stood back-to-back waving their flashlights in the darkness to cover more territory.

"There!" he said. "Is that her?"

They moved in closer with the flashlights reflecting Rosie's eyes. She was whining and not moving.

"Rosie, how are you, girl?" Ida noticed she was wounded.

"Her legs," GG said. "It appears that she's been in a fight of some sort, likely with another animal."

"Can she walk?"

"I don't think so, Ida. We can probably help her though. Let's get her back to the house."

Ida agreed and prayed that they did not encounter whatever animal it was that Rosie had combatted.

GG guessed that her lower legs were fractured, but didn't attempt to set them onsite. He decided, instead, to immobilize them. With Ida holding the flashlights, he removed his shoes and socks so he could use the socks for padding. He then placed branches alongside Rosie's legs so they would not move. The makeshift splints went from above her joints at her hind legs down to her paws to offer her maximum stability. He used Ida's socks to wrap the splints, securing them enough to stop the bleeding and transport her, but not so much that they cut off circulation. Careful not to move her legs any more than necessary, he gingerly picked her up to carry her home.

Ida was not sure that she knew the fastest route back to Patty's house, but they could see the smoke from the chimney and were thankful that it served as a guide. "You're amazing," she said to GG.

Carrying Rosie cradled like an infant he replied, "Thanks, but not really. She's only stabilized, not healed. I'm hoping she's strong enough to assist with Patty's search. If both her hind legs are broken, she may not be able to help much.

They had only hiked about 20 yards when Rosie began to growl. Her tail stood straight up. GG stopped walking and said softly and slowly, as if gritting his teeth while speaking, "Ida, turn off the flashlights."

In her truest, fast-paced tone but with understandable, rational panic, "Oh my God. Oh my God. GG, is that a bear?"

"Shhh. Yes. I think it's a black bear. Slowly, lower yourself to the ground."

Rosie's growl was persistent, but she did not bark. She was weakening and could no longer fight. Still holding her, GG lowered himself to the ground as well.

"We should run for it, GG," Ida whispered.

"No. We cannot outrun him. You wouldn't happen to have capsaicin, would you?"

"What?" She'd never heard of it.

"Pepper spray. Bear spray," he said calmly.

She was shocked, "You mean bear repellant? That's some Batman stuff. You mean, like I should have shark repellant and bear repellant on my person?"

He was not trying to insult her, but was astounded that she had no idea about how to avoid being eaten by a black bear, here, in Shenandoah Valley. "Just a thought—because you have been out here in the woods with Patty. I supposed you would know that black bears are prevalent here and you might have a small survival kit with you."

"Well. Do you have bear repellant?" She tested.

The bear was still sitting there. Not moving. Not growling. Just looking in their direction. GG didn't know if it were silently stalking them and planning an attack. Not sure what else to try, he declared, "We have to try to intimidate it."

"Intimidate it? Are you serious right now? Us? Intimidate a bear? It's a bear."

"Yes, Ida, it is. I will put Rosie down and you and I will pick up rocks, sticks, all that we can grab and throw them at it while screaming loudly. It may be deterred from attacking us if we are aggressive."

"I can't," she answered.

"We have to," he insisted. "If it's stalking us, planning to feed and store up for hibernation, we have to try to scare it."

He lowered Rosie, who was limp and unresponsive, to the ground and said, "On three, we stand up, make noise, and attack. One... two..."

"Wait," she interrupted the count. "What if it moves, we cannot see it?"

"OK. We'll each hold a flashlight in one hand and fight like hell with the other. Don't forget to make noise, aggressive, not helpless. One... two... three."

With their flashlights pointed toward the bear, they stood tall, roaring, throwing rocks and sticks. They had only lasted a few seconds when the bear stood up on its hind feet and bellowed an angry, thunderous roar. Frightened, they continued to attack.

The bear lowered its front legs and began to move slowly toward them. They couldn't find anything else to throw but continued to yell at it. Their efforts were futile. After just a slight trot it had arrived at GG. Ida was hiding behind him and her yell had changed to a scream. She knew they were about to be mauled. She would have prayed, but she couldn't compile a prayer at that moment. All she could muster out was, "Jesus."

With its mouth open wide, it would engulf GG's head in one bite. Not being a very religious person, he didn't know what to pray at that moment either so as he heard Ida shouting "Jesus," he joined her. Screaming that name as loudly as they could still did not deter the animal. It lunged toward GG, ready to feed. With its mouth fully stretched, it moved toward GG's head. Just before it could engulf his head and lock its jaws down to complete the decapitation, there was a loud boom. Then there was another one. Both echoed throughout the mountains.

There was illumination. Ida finally opened her eyes, looked directly into the light, and was blinded by the brightness. "Oh my God, we're dead! I see the light. Do you see it? GG, are we dead?"

Standing, also looking toward the light, he said, "No, Ida. That's a flood light." He began to call out, "Hello. Who's there?" He and Ida shone their lights toward the bright light, but couldn't see anything.

Someone answered GG, "Hello. Are you OK? Is it down?"

GG yelled back, "Yes. We're fine. The bear is down."

The couple moved toward GG and Ida. "Stay put. We are coming to you. Just stay put." They continued to talk to keep GG and Ida calm.

Their voices sounded familiar to GG. He knew these people. As they approached he recognized them. "The Goodleafs."

"Yes. GG and Ida, right?"

Ida had finally composed herself and found words. "How do you know us? And, thank you. Thank you so much. You saved our lives, but wait, how do know our names?"

"Slow down," said Mrs. Goodleaf. "Breathe." We live on the property next door. After the earthquake and power outage, we set out to check on our neighbors. Patty is the only one we hadn't been able to reach, so we went to her house. Estelle told us you were out here searching for Rosie, so we came to help.

"Yes, she's here," GG said and pointed down to the listless animal. She's injured. I made splints and was attempting to bring her to the house, but we encountered that," he pointed to the bear still somewhat in disbelief that his head had just been seconds away from entering into that creature's mouth. "Thank you for coming. Thank you."

"No worries," Mr. Goodleaf said. He checked to see if Rosie were still breathing. She was, but her eyes were closed. He retrieved a large cloth folded in his backpack and wrapped it around his left shoulder to make a carrying pouch. GG, still shaking, lifted Rosie from the ground and placed her in Mr. Goodleaf's provisional sling. Up close to Mr. Goodleaf and getting a close look at him, GG marveled at what a stereotypical mountain man he was. His face was hidden underneath long, unkempt hair and a remarkably wild, long, white beard; nevertheless, this mountain man and his wife had just saved them from being eaten by a bear and he would be forever grateful.

Mr. Goodleaf supported Rosie with his left arm and hand, and wrapped his right arm around GG. "You're OK now. Let's go."

Looking back at the bear, Mr. Goodleaf declared to it, "He'll make fine stew."

GG couldn't help himself but mock, "Now who's eating who?"

Mrs. Goodleaf was still holding the .300 Winchester Magnum 26" barrel rifle. She was clearly an expert and comfortable firing a bolt action rifle. She carried it in her right hand, held the flood light with her left hand, and warmly guided Ida. "Wrap your arm around my waist. You're fine now."

Ida cherished her timeliness, her precision, and her care and concern.

11: Nurturing

Estelle and Evelyn were attending to Lewis who was weakening by the minute. They had finished making phone calls for search assistance for Patty. Some of the cell towers still must have been affected because they couldn't reach many people, including Ralph.

Mrs. Harris had taken the cooked food out of the oven and placed more food in it. There was more than they would consume, but it gave her something to do to pass the time. She and Estelle had already filled water bottles and gathered supplies in the living room. The Goodleafs had put a generator on their truck in case the power went out again, so that was another threat eradicated. They had also brought warm cider, homemade with apples from their orchards.

Lewis was drifting off to sleep by the fire when Evelyn checked on him again.

"Are you comfortable, Dear?" she asked. "Would you prefer to lie in the bed?"

With his eyes still closed he responded, "Actually, mother, that sounds pretty good. Could you help me?"

Estelle sat her mug on the coffee table and jumped up. "I can help."

He was too weak to stand on his own, so they lifted him. With little struggle, they were able to get him into his wheelchair. Estelle placed his feet on the footrests and brought his blanket. She pushed the chair while Evelyn gathered the IV, oxygen, and monitors, all on wheels, and rolled them alongside him. Together they successfully moved him to the room where Ralph had placed the luggage.

Estelle checked his charts. It was not yet time for medication, but she realized that it had been several hours since he'd eaten. "Can I get you something to eat, Baby? Crackers, cheese, a sandwich, soup, anything?"

"I'm not really hungry, Ma'am, but thank you."

"You should take in something," she insisted. "The apple cider is delicious. Made from the Goodleafs' local orchards and cellars. How about a sip?"

"OK. I'd like that," he agreed.

Evelyn sat on the bed beside Lewis while Estelle went to the kitchen. Realizing he was probably too weak to hold a mug, she poured it in a bowl and brought it to him with a spoon. When she got back to the bedroom, Evelyn reached for the bowl and spoon and held it while Estelle propped Lewis up with pillows. They were synchronized in all their efforts.

"Thank you, Estelle," he said gratefully. "Could I ask one more favor please?"

"Sure, Baby."

"Could you check my phone? It's in the living room by the sofa table. See if there's any news from GG or Patty?"

"Yes, I can." She left the room presuming that Lewis and his mother had not shared many private moments together. Perhaps an opportunity had presented for them to have a little quality, mother-son time.

Not that familiar with cellular phones, Estelle pressed the home button, the only button, on Lewis' phone and the screen lit up. There were lots of icons and some had red numbers on them. *Pandora, App Store, LinkedIn, Mail, Messages,* and *Messenger. How on earth will I know where to check for news on Patty or from GG? she thought.*

She would have taken the phone to him to ask, but that was not his request. He did not ask her to bring him his phone, but rather to check it for him. He may not have felt like checking it for himself or maybe he wanted time alone with his mother. Estelle began to press the icons and explore.

She opened his text messages. There were no new communications regarding Patty. There was a text message from his assistant informing him that his urgent request had been answered in email. *If it's urgent*, Estelle thought, *it might pertain to Patty*. She opened the e-mail app. There were several messages to scroll through. After passing a couple of dozen messages, she saw one with the subject, *RE: Urgent/Trace Family*.

When she opened the message and clicked on the link, Estelle was surprised to see a family tree. It was interactive, so selecting names and branches revealed details of the family line. *This cannot be right*, she thought, *how can this be?* She studied every section of the family tree.

Evelyn was spoon-feeding the warm cider to Lewis. Her hands shook slightly and she sniffled while trying to steady herself. "I didn't know," she said.

"I just found out."

"Will you be OK?" she asked him.

"No."

"How long?" She began to cry.

"Not long. Soon, Mother."

She placed the bowl and spoon on the nightstand and laid her head on his chest. As she began to sob uncontrollably, he tenderly stroked her hair and attempted to console her. "Mother, it'll be OK. We still have now. Here and now."

"Are you scared?"

"Yes, a little."

"Are you praying, Lewis?"

"All the time, Mother."

"He's listening."

"I know. And He's allowing me to see my family again. We will find Patty and I'll get to see my family together again. He's answering my prayers."

"GG seems nice. Is he kind?"

"Yes, he is."

"Good. I'm glad you have him." She smiled.

"Are you, Mother? Are you glad I have GG?"

"Of course, I am, Lewis. Why would you ask that?"

"It's OK." He attempted to dismiss the remark.

"No, it isn't. I want to know. Please. Tell me about him. How did you meet?"

"Mother, we don't have to. Really, it's OK."

"Lewis, I'd love to have this conversation, but only if you want to share. If not, I understand."

"OK, Mother. Let me rest for a bit and I'll give you all the details." He smiled as he drifted off.

She agreed.

Watching him sleep, so many questions ran through her mind. She wondered if the cigar smoking caused his illness. She had known about it for years, smelling it on him occasionally, but never said anything. She also questioned how long he'd had that cough and if catching it earlier would have given him a fighting chance. It saddened her that she couldn't make it better for him. What troubled her most was that she had allowed so much distance to come between them.

Lewis began to grimace as if he were in pain when an alarm went off on the monitor. Estelle heard the alarm from the living room and brought the medicine bag. Evelyn was dazed and disheartened, anxiously longing to know more about her son before it was too late.

After administering his evening dose and making him as comfortable as possible, they quietly left the room, turning off the light and closing the door behind them. Just outside the door,

Evelyn's legs destabilized and buckled. Estelle caught her, preventing her fall. Unable to walk, she leaned on Estelle as she slid down the wall to sit on the floor, and wept.

Estelle was holding Lewis' phone. She needed to discuss her discovery with Evelyn who was in no condition at that moment. Estelle elected instead to provide support and comfort; the news would have to wait a little longer. At that moment, they were lamenting the awful fate of Lewis, Evelyn's son, Estelle's nephew.

12: Secrets

Estelle and Evelyn were relaxing on the sofa when the Goodleafs called Patty's house to inform them that they had found GG, Ida, and Rosie, and were headed back down the mountain. They asked if Estelle could call Dr. Pete, the veterinarian, because Rosie was wounded and she would need medical attention in order to participate in the search for Patty.

The Goodleafs would take 15-20 minutes to meander back down the mountain at that time of night and it would take the same amount of time for Dr. Pete to arrive. That gave Estelle a window of opportunity to converse with Evelyn.

They had finally made it back to kitchen and were eating some of the prepared party food when Estelle suggested they have wine as well. She picked up the bottle Ida had left on the side table, but it was empty so they opened a new one.

They were remarking on the great effort to which Patty had gone to plan and arrange both dinner and the party. The hors d'oeuvres were delicious. Crostini, grilled scallops wrapped in bacon, stuffed peppers with goat cheese, crab salad canapés, and mini crab cakes were just the starters. They were sitting on the sofa together sampling the appetizers when Estelle poured wine for them and found the nerve to start the conversation.

"Evelyn, I discovered something very interesting this evening and I was hoping we could talk about it."

Not really comfortable with anyone other than her husband calling her "Evelyn," she winced a little, but was intrigued about the discovery. She didn't speak, but gave Estelle a nod of approval to continue.

"I was raised by my mother, here in the valley," Estelle began tenderly. "Her name was Emily. My father, I was told, was in the Army. They met when he was stationed nearby. She had hoped he would return and they would marry and be a family. That never happened."

Evelyn was unsure of where the conversation was going, but politely replied, "How tragic. I'm sorry."

"Yes, thank you," Estelle continued. "If I may ask, what was your upbringing like?"

"Well, I don't usually discuss it much." She seemed a little uncomfortable, but there was something about Estelle that relaxed her, so she indulged. "I was raised in New York by both my parents. Like yours, my father was in the military. I suppose that's why he chose Patrick for me."

"Chose?" Estelle inquired. "As in an arranged marriage?"

Somewhat insulted, "Well, that sounds a little barbaric. My father appreciated Patrick's many fine qualities and knew that he would be a good provider and protector for me. He was right."

Apologetically, Estelle explained, "I did not mean to insult you. I should choose my words more carefully." After a nod of acceptance from Evelyn, Estelle asked her please to continue.

"Patrick is a good husband and father. We love our children. I'm fully aware of your special bond with Patricia. She speaks very highly of you. Thank you for caring for her."

"I love Patty," Estelle clarified.

Evelyn continued, "and your apparent instincts regarding Lewis are noted."

Estelle couldn't tell if Evelyn were jealous of her relationship with Patty, and now Lewis, or if she were just responding properly, expressing the appropriate gratitude. She changed the subject back to Evelyn's childhood. "You said you were raised by both your parents?"

Baffled as to why that would seem so remarkable, Evelyn looked her in the eyes and answered with a curt, "Yes."

The conversation was not going as well as Estelle had hoped. Time was winding down and everyone would be back soon, so she had to get to the point.

"When I was checking Lewis' phone earlier for updates on Patty, I discovered something. He had apparently conducted an ancestry trace and it revealed his family tree. I'd like to show it to you."

"His family tree?"

"Yes."

Still not clear on where Estelle was headed with this, Evelyn agreed with her head nod. When Estelle picked up Lewis' phone, they both reached for their reading eyeglasses, the same style, and put them on at the same time.

"If we start at the bottom of the tree, this is Patty's and Lewis' generation. The next level up is your generation and then your parents and grandparents. Let's start with your parents."

Evelyn did her signature single nod of approval. Estelle continued, your parents were John and Margaret Scott."

"Yes."

"OK. Let's click on their block." Estelle waited while Evelyn read the details.

"Wait. This cannot be. Margaret was my stepmother, not my biological mother? According to these dates, she met and married my father after I was born?"

"Keep reading, Evelyn."

"Emily? Didn't you say that your mother's name was Emily and your father, like mine, was in the Army?"

Gulping the red wine, "Keep reading, Evelyn."

"It branches off. Emily's tree goes in a different direction. I see. It's because John and Emily were not married."

"Keep reading, Evelyn."

After a few seconds of silence, Evelyn put the phone on the coffee table. In unison, they took their eyeglasses off and in the most synchronized fashion, slowly turned their heads to face each other. They couldn't believe it. Emily Ann had twin girls who were separated at birth, Evelyn Ann and Estelle Ann.

Simultaneously, they said, "We're twins."

Their reunion was truncated by the commotion. There was a banging at the door. The phone was ringing and there was some sort of ruckus with Lewis down the hall.

Evelyn ran to the bedroom to Lewis. He had fallen and was struggling to get back up. It scared his mother. "Are you OK? What's happening?" she asked him.

With a barely audible whisper, "I thought I could make it to the bathroom."

A machine had come unplugged and was alarming. One of them, perhaps the same one, was dripping on the floor. She tried, but he was too heavy for her to lift him alone. She would have called Estelle for help, but Estelle was answering the door and the phone. Evelyn pulled the covers off the bed, wrapped them around Lewis, and elevated his head enough to slide a pillow underneath.

She sat on the floor and held and rocked him, "Let's just wait here a few minutes, Lewis. Let's just wait together."

Estelle opened the door and waved them inside carrying Rosie while she ran to get the phone. If there were any news of Patty, she didn't want to miss it. Maybe Ned and Rev. Harris had something to report. By the time she reached the phone, the ringing had stopped. She'd have to figure out how to check the call log or caller ID or whatever that darn feature was called. Then there was another knock at the door. Dr. Pete had arrived. Thank God.

GG scanned the room and didn't see Lewis. "Where is he?" He panicked. "Where's Lewis?"

Estelle pointed down the hall, "In the room."

While GG ran to Lewis, the Goodleafs were trying to decide where to place Rosie. Dr. Pete suggested clearing space on a table where he could work. The food covered Patty's dining and coffee tables, so they used the piano.

Ida picked up the half-full wine bottle that Estelle and Evelyn had started. She poured some into one of the glasses that was still there from the sisters' conversation. "There was a bear. We were nearly attacked by a bear." She wasn't speaking to anyone in particular, just loud, fast, and still terrified. "I said, we were almost attacked by a bear. It almost bit off GG's head!"

Estelle responded to her, "I'm glad you're OK." Then, dismissing that conversation, she held up Patty's phone and asked Ida, "How do I check missed calls?"

Flabbergasted, Ida repeated, "We were nearly attacked by a bear."

"Yes, Baby. I'm glad you're OK. I need to know who just called."

"Called?"

"Yes, Ida. Someone was calling when I was opening the door and I missed it. How can I tell who it was?"

"Um, OK," she was about to sip the wine when Estelle took it from her hand.

"Please, Ida. Who was calling? Ned? The authorities?"

"Ned. Ned called. Here, press this button and it will redial him."

After Estelle pressed the redial button, Ida took her wine glass from and went back to the sofa. "We were almost attacked by a bear. It tried to bite off GG's head. No one cares? A bear. A real, live bear."

She began to scroll through the messages on her phone, hoping desperately to find something from Patty, but there was mostly junk mail. After deleting several messages, she came across one that she hadn't expected. "Interesting," she said aloud as she opened a message from Lewis' assistant. He had requested that she include Ida when sending her findings of the ancestry search.

Dr. Pete used one of the jugs of distilled water to rinse Rosie's wounds. He then cleaned them with anti-bacterial soap and warm water and used tweezers to remove small debris from both her legs. Her blood was trickling, but not spurting so he determined that there was probably no severe damage to a blood vessel.

Talking sweetly to Rosie as if she were an injured child, he was just about to administer a sedative before suturing, when he became curious about her collar. "A new collar?" he asked.

Ida still reading the family tree on her phone, lifted her head to say, "Yes. I designed it."

"How does it work?" Dr. Pete inquired.

Ida explained that it was linked to Patty's bracelet and they were hoping that Rosie could be helpful with the search and rescue.

"I'm glad you expounded. I was just about to sedate her. I'll use a local anesthetic instead."

GG was helping Lewis. He was back and forth between the bedroom and bathroom, in and out of his black bag, and moving frantically. Estelle and Evelyn had offered to help, but he politely asked them for privacy and assured them that everything was under control. After several minutes, he came back up to the living room with several items tied in a garbage bag for disposal.

"Is Lewis OK?" Evelyn and Estelle asked him in unison.

"Yes, he's resting comfortably." GG noted for the first time a striking resemblance in the two ladies. They looked and sounded a lot alike.

"Are you OK?" Ida asked. She was amazed that the man who had just been attacked by a bear had not mentioned it once because he was consumed with caring for his friend. She marveled at his character and how selfless and loving and affectionate he was.

"I'm fine." He sounded exhausted. Holding the garbage bag a little higher, he said, "I just need to take this out. I'll be right back."

He took the waste out to Patty's trashcans on the side of her house. He was just about to turn and come inside when his legs weakened. Dropping to his knees, he cupped his hands together, laid his face in them, and cried. The thought of losing Lewis so soon was so painful that GG couldn't stand it. It would've been easier to die at the mouth of that bear than to say goodbye to Lewis.

Estelle was on the phone with Rev. Harris who wanted to know if Rosie had been located. She described Rosie's condition to him and he wanted to know if she were alert enough to come to the search location. Dr. Pete confirmed that she was alert, but cautioned that she should not put any weight on her hind legs. She'd have to be carried.

"Understood," Rev. Harris said. "Bring her. Bring Ida. Pronto." He hung up.

Dr. Pete announced that they wanted Rosie at the search site, but he had a prior commitment. The Goodleafs offered to take her. They removed the cover from the piano, folded it, and added a pillow to pad an empty wine crate. They would use that to transport her to the school.

"He also said to bring Ida," Dr. Pete repeated the command.

"OK. I'll ride with you," Ida said to the Goodleafs.

At that moment, GG entered. "What's going on?" he inquired.

"We're taking Rosie to help with the search for Patty," she explained.

"I'm coming, too," he said. "I'll go tell Lewis."

As GG ran to Lewis' room, the Goodleafs and Ida were heading out to the truck. He emerged with Lewis in a wheelchair.

"What are you doing?" Estelle and Evelyn asked him, in harmony.

"I'm going to help search for my sister," Lewis declared. His tone suggested that his decision was not open for discussion.

Lewis' machines were still on, but unplugged and using battery power. Because they had been unplugged for a while earlier that evening, the batteries were not fully charged. He had two large bags hanging on the sides of his wheelchair. They had approached the door to exit the house when he paused, retrieved his camera from one of the bags, and looked up to take a picture of Evelyn and Estelle. They had escorted him to the door, were holding one another, and sharing the same worried grimace.

13: Searching

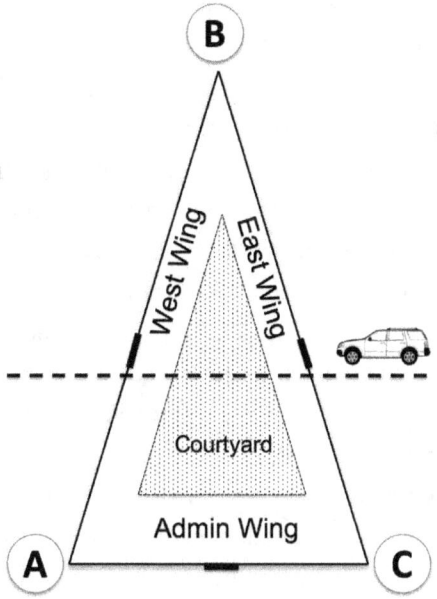

On route to the school, Ned considered having a man-to-man chat with Rev. Harris. He had heard much about Rev. Harris from Patty, but had never spoken with him directly. His attempts were all futile.

"So, Mr. Harris..." he tried.

He was interrupted, "I prefer to be addressed as Reverend Harris, General Harris, or Sir."

"Duly noted," he began again. "Rev. Harris, I think Patty is a very special person..."

Interrupted again, "I know that my daughter is special."

"Yes, Sir." He realized that Rev. Harris was not open to conversation just yet.

The solemn 15-minute drive felt like several hours, but they finally arrived at the school and were astounded to find it leveled. Completely flattened. Both floors on all three sides of the building had collapsed. It was practically unidentifiable. There was no structure. There was no courtyard.

It was also late evening in the valley and, therefore, cold. The sun had set and the power surge had affected the parking lot lights, so there was no illumination of the campus.

"Circle the building," Rev. Harris instructed Ned. He wanted to assess the complete site. They drove slowly across the front of the building. Ned explained that she would not be in that area because it was the admin wing. She was entering on the east wing side, close to the music room.

They turned into the west wing parking lot. It too was demolished. Ned continued to explain to Rev. Harris, who did not speak at all between commands, that Patty's classroom was on the second floor.

"Where would she park?" he inquired.

"Normally, here, on the east wing, but the doors were locked this evening. The only unlocked door was on the west wing. She would have parked there and then walked to her classroom."

Continuing their site assessment, they turned into the west wing parking lot.

Ned drove slowly looking for Patty's green truck in the dark. As he approached the middle of the wing, he saw it. "There!" he yelled. He anxiously pulled up to Patty's truck and parked beside it.

Jumping out of Ned's truck, they each ran to check for unlocked doors. No luck. They were all locked. Cupping their hands against the windows they were able to peek inside, only seeing her purse and her wrap. They looked up at each other and then at the collapsed building. Simultaneously, they nodded. They knew she was buried underneath all the wreckage.

Worse than he had imagined and far more emotional than any combat he'd ever experienced, Rev. Harris stood solemn, looking toward the piles of debris. All those years of combat command and military training, his service as a chaplain and now as a pastor, did not prepare him for this. *How on earth could this have happened? A building has collapsed on my daughter.*

Rev. Harris's eyes welled full. It was unfathomable that God had allowed such a tragedy. How could He have brought me through so much, but allowed this to happen to my child? Why would he allow this? Patricia has worked here for 20 years safely, happily, with no problems, and on the night of her retirement celebration, He did this. Why here? Why now? Why on the day of my first visit to her? Why, God? His emotions were a dangerous combination of fear and anger.

Ned interrupted his thought and called for his attention, "Rev. Harris. Sir. Rev. Harris."

"Yes?"

"Sir, she's here. Let's find our girl."

Still deep in thought and attempting to process what he was seeing, he nodded in agreement. That gesture was an affirmation of their joint mission.

Ned went back to his truck and retrieved his iPad. There was a blueprint of the building, the one his team used for safety drills. He began to brief Rev. Harris. "We are here," he said as he pointed to a tiny spot on the map at the center of the outside of the west wing.

Then sliding his finger forward slightly to the inside of the same corridor, "The music room is here."

"She would have entered this door on the first floor. We don't know which way she went. Our security team refers to each of the three vertices by alphabet: A, B, and C. Here we are between B and C. Her classroom is between A and B, on the second floor. The courtyard was closed off so the shortest path to her classroom would be to go up the east wing to B, turn left, and then go halfway down the corridor. She's most likely somewhere between the midpoints of A/B and B/C. That defines our search zone."

Rev. Harris had discovered respect for Ned. "Then that's our target area." He had Ned call Patty's house to ascertain how much help Estelle had rounded up, but the call went to voicemail. "For now, let's split up. You start at A/B and I'll start at B/C.

They were just about to get started when a truck pulled up. It was Ned's security team coming to help search for Patty.

"Estelle called us, Sir. There's not much help. It's just us," one of them said to Ned. "The quake and the power outages have all of our emergency and medical services tied up. What can we do?"

"Thanks. I appreciate it. We think she's between A/B and B/C so that's where we'll search."

"How many radios do we have?" Rev. Harris questioned.

"We each have one, Sir."

Rev. Harris had a plan. "There are six of us. Two of you start where we know she entered the building, at B/C. The outsides of the wings are longer than the insides, so we need more effort on the outside. Not knowing names, he pointed as he directed, first to the security officers and then to their post on the blueprint.

"You, start here at B/C and go outside north toward B." To the next, "You, start here at B and come southward outside to B/C. The two of you will meet at the halfway point." They were the East Wing Outside Team.

To the third officer, "You, start here at A/B and go outside north toward B." To the fourth, "You, start here at B and come southward outside to A/B. The two of you will meet at the halfway point." They comprised the West Wing Outside Team.

"Ned and I will start inside the corridors on the courtyard side at B. Ned, you search inside from A to B. I will search inside from C to B. We will meet at inside B."

His additional directives, "Try not to make noises. If she's conscious, she might make movements or sounds. Only use your radio when you find her."

The building was more than 90,000 square feet, so the task ahead was daunting. Because they were only searching half of the premises and it had only collapsed a few hours ago, they were optimistic.

The building clearly did not have a good foundation and could not withstand the vibrations of the ground. Excess water has always been an issue in the valley. The earthquake must have caused the liquefied sand and excess water to force their way to the ground surface from several meters below the ground.

The windows, while providing access to the scenic views, were not a sound structural idea. Mixed in with broken slabs of concrete, sheetrock, bricks, furniture, water pipes, electrical wires, and tires was an enormous amount of broken glass.

This mission was one of search and rescue. First, they'd have to find Patty and then they'd have to dig her out.

Thankfully, there were only two floors. That made the search less vertical. The corridors, however, were so long that searching foot by foot would take several hours and time was not luxury for these teams. It was dark and cold, and they had no idea what physical state Patty was in, if she were still alive.

They were starting toward their posts when a large truck pulled into the parking lot. The Goodleafs had arrived with Rosie and were accompanied by Ida, GG, and Lewis.

Mr. Goodleaf was carrying Rosie. Mrs. Goodleaf began unloading equipment: what looked like a state-of-the-art tent, flood lights, a couple of generators, water, trays of food, and blankets. GG was helping Lewis with machines and bags and his wheelchair. Ida was holding a bottle of wine.

Rev. Harris would have commented on the apparent dysfunction of this misfit group, but for now, he was grateful for any assistance they could get and, it seemed, there was no more help coming any time soon.

To Mr. Goodleaf, "Who are you? Grizzly Adams?"

Ignoring the acerbity, "I'm Patty's neighbor." He pointed to Mrs. Goodleaf. "She's my wife." He, too, had heard many stories of Rev. Harris over the years and was not a fan, as was evident by his ever-so-blunt responses.

He continued, "Rosie has been injured. She's alert, but cannot put any weight on her hind legs."

Rev. Harris looked at GG who was standing next to Lewis and sounded exasperated. "Why did you bring him here?"

GG's response was also terse. "He wanted to come."

Lewis began to retrieve cameras from his bags and announced, "I'm not strong enough to search or dig for Patty, but I can photograph her story."

"You're not strong enough, Junior."

"I will photo journal my sister's rescue."

From his wheelchair, with GG's assistance, Lewis began assembling his equipment.

Rev. Lewis looked at Ida and this time resisted the urge to comment on her exposed cleavage or the wine bottle in her hand. "Tell me how the collar works."

She was articulate in briefing him. "Patty is wearing a bracelet. When she presses a button once, it sends a signal to Rosie's collar. It's similar to a dog whistle: Rosie can hear it, but we cannot.

She'll also feel a slight vibration. The ultra-sonic sound and vibration will attract Rosie to Patty's bracelet."

"What's the greatest distance it will work between Patty's bracelet and Rosie's collar?"

"Approximately 50 yards."

"Can we use this to initiate communication with Patty?"

"No. Patty initiates communication with Rosie. In addition, Patty can press and hold another button and speak. If Rosie is within 20 feet, she can also hear Patty's voice through the speaker on her collar."

"How is it powered?"

"It's solar powered, lasting about 48 hours. It was fully charged when I picked it up from my jeweler in Jersey this morning."

He looked at Ida and smiled for the first time since he'd been on this trip. "Perfect."

He then took the wine bottle from her hand and took a big gulp from the bottle before handing it back to her. He was pleased indeed. Lewis captured that moment with photos.

Rev. Harris called out to Ned's officers, "We need a bullhorn and a wheelbarrow."

"We have a wheelbarrow," one of the officers answered him.

"I have a bullhorn," another shouted out.

That was all they needed. He updated the security officers with the modified plan. "We'll call out for Patricia as we search, informing her that Rosie is here and we need her to push the button on her bracelet so we can locate her."

"Sir," one of the officers questioned, "we only have one bullhorn. Do we take turns using it?"

"No, son. We'll place Rosie in a wheelbarrow center point of our search area, not to exceed 50 yards in any direction. Take your posts and turn on your radios to receive transmission. Ned will have his radio on as he calls out for Patricia through the bullhorn. His calls out to her will broadcast throughout our search perimeter through your radios. All Patricia has to do is transmit the signal when she hears him. Rosie's response to the signal will lead us to Patricia's location. Ned will continue to communicate to her through the bullhorn and radios. Once we are within 20 feet, Patricia can also communicate with us verbally."

"Genius!" Ida screeched. "Pure, freaking genius."

14: Reunion

Back at Patty's house, Ned had been calling Evelyn and Estelle periodically to update them on the search. There hadn't been any new developments since discovering Patty's truck but communication was crucial. He could ease their anxiety with routine situation reports. More importantly, he had Estelle relay those updates to search and rescue personnel should they be able to assist.

Ned had recently inquired about a Crew Leader position with the Department of Emergency Management. To better qualify, he had to complete a two-part training program. Part One of the training comprised learning response to help locate a lost or missing person. It mostly focused on missing children and wandering dementia subjects. Part Two was Search and Rescue. That is where he learned to search for victims who were stranded or trapped in collapsed structures or fallen debris. That training, in addition to his knowledge of the campus, eased the anxiety that Estelle would have had otherwise. She was as confident in Ned's ability to find and save Patty as Evelyn was in Rev. Harris' skills to accomplish the same.

Evelyn was aware of his experiences in uniting and detailing men and women for critical tasks. If anyone could establish a group and organize them to find to Patty, it was her husband.

The sisters agreed that if any two people could rescue Patty, it would be her dad and her fiancé. Of course, no one knew that Ned and Patty were engaged yet. She had hoped to break the news to them at her retirement party.

With the search party in full effect, Ida's role was to relieve Estelle and take over communications. It was more efficient because she was onsite with the search team. She became the point of contact for emergency services. The local police, the U.S. Coast Guard, the fire department, the American Red Cross, and all other organizations that Estelle had contacted for help were given Ida's cell phone number. So far, none would arrive for at least another 6 to 8 hours.

That would be Saturday morning, so Rev. Harris planned for the team to search all night until the next crew arrived. They could rotate out for short breaks underneath the supply tent. Mrs. Goodleaf had set up all they needed to sustain, including food and drinks that Patty had purchased for the dinner party. There was even the crockpot of spicy chili she had made for Ida's arrival. In actuality, there were enough supplies to last the team for several days, but they were all praying for a much shorter search and rescue.

Now that the sisters were up-to-date, relieved of some of their responsibilities, and assured that Patty would be found, they could finally have their conversation. There were so many secrets that their family tree had revealed. The biggest, obviously, was that John and Emily Ann had twin girls, who were separated at birth.

Evelyn had only known Margaret as "Mom," a lovely lady with a mild demeanor. She had wonderful memories of growing up with nurturing, caring parents who lived together in Manhattan until he passed away. She could not fathom them keeping such a secret from her. She wondered why they hadn't told her such an important detail about her heredity. She never got to know her biological mother and that now raised so many questions. *What was she like? Why did she separate her twins? How did she decide which to keep?*

She had never questioned why she didn't resemble Margaret physically because she had all of her father's prominent features. She had his small eyes, flat nose, high cheek bones, brown skin, wide smile, and long legs. She had Margaret's mannerisms. They had extraordinarily similar gestures, habits, behaviors, and routines. They even had the same soft, quiet laugh. It became obvious, however, those were a result of nurturing and influence much more than genetics.

Estelle's upbringing was in stark contrast. She grew up in a single-parent home, with her mother alone. There had been little discussion of her father. On the rare occasion when she inquired of his existence or whereabouts, Emily Ann would only say that he was in the Army. Estelle didn't know if he were dead or alive, if he knew about her, and if so, if he cared to know her. His absence in her life created a void and her mother realized it, so Emily Ann went out of her way to make life pleasant for Estelle.

Emily Ann had many talents, the greatest of which was music. She was the church pianist and she taught music lessons to children in their community to earn extra money. Estelle was among the many pupils who had learned to play the piano and organ under her tutelage.

Estelle's home, while modest in size and appearance, was filled with history. It had been her mother's childhood home as well. Estelle's grandmother Emma had left the house to her only daughter Emily. When Emily passed away, she had willed the house to Estelle. Three generations of church-going, piano teaching, unmarried women had made that little cottage a warm and loving home.

Estelle had often wished that she'd had a daughter to continue the tradition. It hadn't worked out that way. The closest she had come was her bond with Patty. The new discovery explained their instant connection. For 20 years, they had shared their love of mountain life. Could it have been more than fate that brought Patty back Shenandoah Valley? They had worked at the same college, shared meals and conversations, all with an inexplicable familial vibe. Estelle had run track when she was in high school and track was Patty's passion. Estelle taught Patty piano just as Grandma Emma taught her daughter, Emily, who taught Estelle. Estelle smiled at the thought of how Patty had learned with such ease—she was a natural.

Estelle now also understood her instant bond with Lewis. He was her nephew. She had heard stories about him over the years from Patty who adored him. Like his sister, he loved oatmeal, wore lots of brown clothes, enjoyed photography, and was fascinated with the sunrise.

But he, unlike his sister, was stylish and trendy. He probably inherited that characteristic from his mother. He was non-confrontational, to his own detriment. Not one to go against the grain, he'd much rather be a peacemaker.

What astounded Estelle most about Lewis was his relationship with GG. She had loved GG like a nephew his entire life and here he was loving and caring for Lewis, her biological nephew, whom she'd never really known.

Estelle turned to Evelyn and held both her hands. "All my life there's been a void. It's always felt as if a part of me were missing. I couldn't explain it."

Evelyn struggled to push the words out, "I know. Me too. I've had a loneliness that I attributed to being an only child. Now I know that I wasn't the only one." She burst into tears.

"And Patty," Estelle continued, "My God. Our Patty. I have loved her since day one. Did you know that her very first day on the job, I fed her? I made her sit down and join me for lunch. The best part of my day, every day, has been Patty. She's everything to me. Do you know she plays piano just like me, like our mother, and our grandmother?"

"Oh Estelle!" She was overjoyed. "I have longed for a piano for years. Patrick won't allow one in the church or in our home. I download music to my phone just to hear the sounds. I have most of the classics, but I listen to something from Chopin or Beethoven every day."

Evelyn had another thought, "and we could not understand what attracted Patricia to Shenandoah Valley. We just couldn't understand the magnetic force it has on her. When we were stationed here when she was in high school—she loved it then."

"Of course she does. She's the fifth generation of us here." She opened the family tree on her phone again and moved her finger along the family tree. "Look at this: Erline was our great grandmother who migrated here with sharecroppers from the south. Ethel was our grandmother. Emily Ann was our mother. You and I are the fourth generation. The only difference with Patricia is her name. Hers doesn't begin with an "E.""

Evelyn looked up from the phone to Estelle. "Actually, it does."

"What do you mean?"

"We named her 'Patricia Erica Ann Harris'. I chose 'Patricia' after Patrick. My father, well, our father, chose her middle names, 'Erica Ann'. I just didn't know why and I felt so strongly about it when she was born."

They decided to stand in front of the mirror, side by side. Noting their remarkable physical similarities was fascinating them.

"I look like Daddy," Evelyn whispered.

"I look like Momma," Estelle said.

"But we look alike," Evelyn was surprised. "Do you have pictures of our mother?"

"I do. Lots of them," Estelle told her. "And our grandmother and great grandmother. You must come by the house."

"I would love that. And I have pictures of Daddy back at home."

"Evelyn, I have so many questions. I wish I could have met him."

"I know. I have questions too. I wish I could have met our mother."

"I know," and then it occurred Estelle again, "I have a sister, a twin sister. And a niece, a nephew, and a brother-in-law. I have a family."

"All these years, I worried about Patty being here without family, she had you."

"Let's call Ida for an update."

15: Photo Journal

GG had taken on two roles during the search. He was still Lewis' attending physician and now he was volunteering as his photography assistant. Medically, he was monitoring Lewis' vital signs, timing his medication dosages, and keeping him hydrated. In his new role, he held reflectors, changed lenses, and uploaded digital files via Wi-Fi SIM cards. Lewis had used online photo albums for organizing and sharing his work and he had GG uploading to a newly created project that he'd named, "Faith." GG worked tirelessly pushing the wheelchair, dispensing medication, and managing the photography equipment: never complaining, never losing patience.

GG borrowed the Goodleafs' truck to drive back to the campus entrance. Lewis' lighting technique was so precise that he was able to use the headlights from the truck, umbrella lights, panel lights, and his arsenal of flashes to photograph in the dark.

The pictures of the front entrance looked as if a deck of cards had collapsed. One layer folded neatly over the next. That must have been an unfurnished area because it consisted mostly of concrete, tile, and drywall.

As he moved across the front of the building to turn and go up the west wing, the debris changed. He captured the business area, information technology labs, and the law library with photos that zoomed in on computers, books, and chairs. The mixture of school equipment with the structural debris precisely depicted nature's interruption of the education that would take place there. His sister's classroom was on the second floor, but that didn't exist anymore.

When they turned again to go down the east wing parking lot, just about midway down the wing, they could see Patty's truck again. He photographed it from a distance at first and from angles that showed the structural damage in the front with her truck faintly in the background. As they moved closer to her truck, it became the focal point of the pictures. It was the last known place where they were certain his sister had been. He then presented the danger. His sister was missing. The close-up pictures illustrated her purse inside, the ignition with no keys, and a full water bottle. Her belongings were there, but she was not.

The inside search area of the courtyard was much smaller than the outside corridors. Ned had completed his area and stayed center court next to Rosie to continue broadcasting calls out to Patty.

Rev. Harris had also concluded searching his assigned area and stationed himself near her truck. He had a folding chair, like those commonly used by spectators at sporting events, and a large travel mug filled with hot coffee, compliments of Mrs. Goodleaf. The mug was larger than the built-in cup holder, so he sat it on the ground beside his chair. The photos portrayed it as a director's seat rather than a spectator's. It was essential to the story. His chair was unoccupied because he was on the field leading, not sitting by idly on the sideline.

Lewis must have taken a hundred photos of his father, who was patrolling the site. Some were of his silhouette. Others captured his concern. Some were close up of the radio in his hand and the ash that covered his shoes. There were others of his eyes squinting and neck stretching to see in the darkness. He showed him walking to and fro, not pacing but intentional, checking the locations of the search teams. The pictures showed him as strong and stable, focused and determined. He was pictured as a fearless leader who would accomplish his mission. He would find his daughter.

Next, he photographed the Goodleafs. They were the Iroquoian neighbors who had been so good to Patty. They had welcomed her into their community and they loved her. They taught her wilderness safety. They shared from their orchards and vineyards. They included her in all of their family events. They were family to her.

His photos did not focus as much on their physical appearance as their wonderful human qualities. Mrs. Goodleaf slowly stirred the pot of chili, neatly folded and stacked blankets, and caringly peeked out toward the building for any sight of news. While caring and thoughtful, however, she was not delicate. Some of the photos showed her shotgun propped up against her chair.

Mr. Goodleaf was less than striking. He wore an overcoat that was made of patchwork and it looked to have been long past its original coloring. He also seemed to be hidden underneath unusually long hair. The original color of it remains uncertain. Those details, however, were not Lewis' points of focus. He concentrated instead on Mr. Goodleaf fueling and maintaining the generators, charging batteries for the radios and flashlights, and stacking jugs of water.

The pop-up tent was impressive. They had set it up in a matter of minutes, but it was not just a 10'x10' canopy. It was a one-room privacy shelter with sidewalls. It was resistant to both water and flame and it zipped for 360° of protection and privacy. Inside, along one wall, the Goodleafs had set up a medical area. There were a couple of cots, some first aid kits, and sterilized equipment.

Lewis also photographed Ida truthfully. He could have snapped shots of a voluptuous woman hanging on tightly to a wine bottle, but that's not who Ida was. His pictures showed her making and receiving phone calls and relaying updates to Rev. Harris. She was their onsite communications liaison. He also captured her intensity as she worked hard to obtain and share information. There were no pictures of the wine bottles and no pictures of her body, as they were not essential to the story.

GG approached Mr. Goodleaf to ask a favor. "Lewis would like to get to the courtyard. Will you help me transport him there? I don't see a way in with the truck."

Not questioning and always happy to oblige, Mr. Goodleaf agreed to help. "Sure. Let's make a path."

They were moving debris to clear enough space for the wheelchair to get through when Rev. Harris noticed them. "What's going on?"

Not looking up from their work, GG answered him, "Lewis wants to go to the courtyard."

Rev. Harris sat his coffee cup by his chair, clipped his radio to his belt, and joined in to help them. Lewis photographed the entire 30 minutes that it took them to clear him a path for him to go out to the courtyard.

He was at the center of the search area where Ned was broadcasting, just beside Rosie in her wheelbarrow. He named the next chapter of photos, "A Wheelchair and a Wheelbarrow." Rosie was still sedated but alert. The light on her collar indicated that it was still charged and they were hoping that very soon she'd respond to a signal from Patty.

Lewis shot pictures of her curled up in the wheelbarrow. Her huge brown ears were floppy and the brown patches around her eyes were separated by a white streak that went down to her neck. Both her legs were bandaged, but Lewis was careful to show that she was more than just some wounded pup. She was a resilient and loyal hound dog, ready and able to help find her owner. Rosie was soon to be a hero.

Realizing there was so much territory to cover even from the courtyard, he decided to use his drone. He was able to capture 4K video and get still shots of the collapsed building and the dispatched search teams. Using a remote control and his tablet, he navigated the drone over the west wing, east wing, and the corridors. The video ended with the drone landing, capturing the wheelchair and the wheelbarrow, and two disabled souls desperately wanting Patty found safely. It was also no mistake that the video showed GG fussing over the medical equipment and the photography equipment as they stood in the center court of the dilapidated building.

Concerned for Lewis' rapidly declining condition, GG decided to take him to the tent. He called Ida and asked her to let the Goodleafs know that Lewis was coming to lie down. She had an incoming call from Estelle and Evelyn at the same time. When she told them about Lewis, they decided to ride over and be with him, bringing more blankets and warm cider from Patty's house.

The sisters had arrived by the time Rev. Harris, Lewis, and GG returned to the tent. They had made the cot with linens and blankets so he'd be comfortable, but he wouldn't agree to lie down just yet. He wanted to make sure that all the photos uploaded to his "Faith" photo journal.

GG agreed, but only after he took pictures of his Auntie E and Evelyn with Lewis. They were so lovingly attentive to him. He wondered if anyone else noticed how much the two ladies looked and sounded alike.

All of the pictures, hundreds of them, had uploaded and Lewis had been tucked in. Mrs. Goodleaf brought a portable heater to his bedside. Mr. Goodleaf plugged the medical machines into the generator to recharge. GG, true to character, double-checked the monitors and intravenous drips. When he kneeled by Lewis to speak to him, the others respectfully stepped outside the tent to give them privacy.

"All the files are uploaded, Lewis. You did it. You're a photo journalist."

Too weak to lift his head or even open his eyes, he corrected GG, "We did it. Thank you so much."

"It's my pleasure. You've dreamt of this for a long time."

"GG, do you have faith?"

"What do you mean?"

Lewis clarified, "in the things you hope for?"

GG held Lewis' hand, "Yes. I do."

"Good." Almost immediately, Lewis drifted off to sleep.

16: Faith and Hope

The continuous broadcast from Ned had drained his officers' radio batteries. He called Ida to inform her that the search team was coming to the tent for a short break, to warm up, get water, and exchange batteries.

Ida made the announcement to everyone already gathered outside the tent. The sisters offered to help Mrs. Goodleaf arrange refreshments for the officers. Rev. Harris would help Mr. Goodleaf distribute fresh batteries and then recharge those turned in, dispense full water bottles, and if any of others needed a longer break, he would stand in for them.

Thinking that GG and Lewis had shared several minutes of privacy, they all re-entered the tent to prepare for the search teams' break. Lewis was asleep on a cot that was parallel to the wall. GG had pulled a cot over beside him, so close that he could lie next to him, almost spooning him. They each had a light blanket and the space heater was near them, but it was so chilly out that Estelle suggested adding another blanket on them. Before anyone else could, Rev. Harris grabbed one, not two, and spread it over the both of them. Evelyn's eyes welled full.

Ned and the other four men were approaching the tent just as all the provisions had been arranged for them. They had seen GG, Lewis, and the drone when they were photographing and wondered what that was all about, but no one asked. As they entered the tent and saw them lying next to one another, they were curious about that as well, but again, respectfully, no one questioned. They exchanged dead batteries for charged ones, nibbled on a few of the refreshments, and then they were ready to head back out for the search. They didn't sit and appeared to be rushing to resume searching. No one had lost sight of their mission and everyone knew that each passing minute was critical.

Evelyn tugged on her husband's arm and requested permission to ask him a question. Once permitted, she asked if they could have a group prayer for their children, Lewis and Patty. One was terminally ill and the other was in grave danger. He agreed.

"Let us pray," he announced and reached for Evelyn's hand on one side and Estelle's on the other.

Forming a semi-circle around GG and Lewis, all the others in the tent joined hands and bowed their heads.

He began, "Father God, we thank you..."

Ida interrupted the prayer, "What's that noise?"

"Ida please," Rev. Harris quieted her.

He began again, "Father God, we thank you..."

Ida interrupted again, "Wait. What is that?"

"Ida. We are praying. A little respect please." His tone was steady but his patience was short.

"I hear it, too," one of the security officers said.

They all stepped outside the tent to listen for it. "Oh my God," Ida shouted, "That's Rosie. She's barking. That's Rosie. Rosie has a signal."

Ned looked to Rev. Harris, "Sir, please pray fast—short and fast."

"Father God, thank you in advance for saving Patricia and blessing Junior. Amen." The others agreed with an "Amen." He, Ned, and the others began to jog toward Rosie in the courtyard. Ida's phone rang. It was the Channel 3 News team.

"We have all the information you've provided and we saw the pictures too. We are broadcasting the photo journal throughout the valley region," the journalist told Ida.

"Pictures? What pictures?" Ida asked.

"Those from Mr. Lewis Harris. His work is impressive."

Ida then realized that GG had shared Lewis' photos with the media. "Yes, Ma'am. He's Patty's brother."

We are en route via helicopter and should arrive in about 15 minutes. We have also asked everyone in the region who is able to search to come to the campus and help. Is there anything else we can do?"

Ida asked the journalist to hold while she checked with Rev. Harris. "Sir, the news station is 15 minutes away via helicopter. They emitted an emergency broadcast for all able bodies in the area to come assist. What else do we need?"

Not needing time to think about it, he answered immediately, "Illumination. Have them hover over Rosie and illuminate the field so we can see."

"Sir, their live broadcast may interfere with your radios' signals," she cautioned him.

"Have them kill their broadcast. We need our radios. All we need from them is light."

Ida switched back over to the journalist on the other line. "Ma'am, we are a few hours away from sunrise and desperately need light. Could you have your helicopter fly over the search site, locate Rosie, the hound in a wheelbarrow, and hover there with lights? The more illumination the better."

"Sure," the journalist obliged.

"We are afraid your broadcast will interfere with our search radios." Ida explained how they were using the radios. "Can you kill your broadcast?" Ida asked.

The journalist offered an alternative. "We have a professional megaphone attached to a speaker system. We can communicate from the air."

Ida was appreciative, "Thank you. I'll inform her dad. Call me when you arrive and he'll have instructions for you."

Ida called Rev. Harris again. "They can use their megaphone and speaker system from their helicopter. They'll call when they arrive for instructions."

"Roger that."

It had been several minutes since Rosie's last howl. The search team was assembled around her waiting for the next response.

Ida was brainstorming. Just as she does at work when designing, she retrieved a notepad from her purse and started diagramming. *Rosie was in the center of a search receiving a signal that could be up to 50 yards away in any direction. They needed to narrow the search area. If the helicopter would instruct Patty to signal in intervals, they could locate her faster. They needed to know when they were getting closer versus moving farther away.*

Minutes later, the helicopter was over the courtyard. Ida was also there with the teams on the ground. When the journalist called, she handed her phone to Rev. Harris.

He had thought it through. When Ned and I searched the inside courtyard, there was no response from Rosie. Assuming Patricia was alert, she did not hear us. Let's rule out the inner corridors for now. The others had not finished searching the outer wings.

He spoke to the journalists. "We'll lift Rosie into the truck and drive along the outer corridors. Patricia parked on the east wing, so let's start there."

"Yes, Sir." There was something about his commanding diction that always produced a respectful response.

"You follow along with us for constant illumination and, every 50 yards, instruct her to signal. Let her know that she is only to signal when you ask for it." He was confident in this tactic.

Rev. Harris then explained to the team that if Patricia were on the other side of the field, Rosie would not receive the signal. When Rosie did receive the signal, they would know that they were moving in the right direction and getting close to her. He ordered them to load Rosie and her wheelbarrow into the pickup truck. He and Ned would bring all the rescue equipment in Ned's truck so that when they found her they'd be prepared to rescue her.

With the helicopter overhead, the pickup truck with Rosie and the security officers just ahead of them, Ned was alone in his truck with Rev. Harris and had to ask him something.

"Sir, may I ask you a question?"

Looking straight ahead and without inflection, "You may."

"How did you know that Patty would transmit a signal?"

Rev. Harris answered, "Faith."

He turned to Ned and asked him, "How do you know she'll still be alive and alert?"

"Hope."

They had driven roughly 50 yards and the helicopter team called out to Patty for a signal, but there wasn't one. They continued to do so along the corridor all the way up to the B vertex. Just as they turned to go down the west wing, they saw a processional of cars and trucks coming toward them. They were halfway down the wing near the location where Patty's classroom would have been and Rosie lifted her head from the wheelbarrow.

The guys in the pickup signaled for their driver to stop. When Ned saw them halt, he did as well. The men and women of the community parked near their stopped trucks. The helicopter team called out for Patty to signal again. Rosie lifted her head again.

This time he gave more specific instructions. He had the officers unload Rosie from the truck and proceed down the wing on foot slowly pushing her wheelbarrow. The airborne team was encouraging Patty to keep signaling because they were getting close. Rosie barked. She had distinct vocalizations. Her bark was different from her howl. She was barking loudly, but intermittently. Something had gotten her attention.

They continued to wheel her, inch by inch. Suddenly, she stretched her neck upward, threw her head back and howled. She made a high-pitched, long mournful sound and she did so repeatedly. As they progressed, Rosie switched to her third vocalization, a cross between a bark and a howl. It was shorter than a howl and it had a sharper, harsher sound. It echoed throughout the campus. Patty had gotten her attention.

The team continued to move in the same direction and then stopped suddenly. They were within 20 feet and could hear Patty's voice. It was faint but it was certain. "Rosie. Rosie. Here, girl."

Rosie stretched her neck toward the center of a huge heap of wreckage. Ned picked her up and began to climb over debris in the direction that Rosie led him. The air team told Patty that the ground team could hear her and would begin her rescue. Rosie had led them to the very spot where Patty was buried.

Ida called back to the tent to let Estelle and Evelyn know that Patty had responded, her location had been discovered, and they were starting to excavate. She also inquired about Lewis' condition.

Rev. Harris split the volunteers into two teams. One would remove debris from the inside tossing it into the courtyard. The other would remove from the outside pitching it toward the parking lot.

Using his bullhorn, he began to speak to Patty as they dug. "Patricia, we are here darling. We can hear you. Are you injured?"

"I think so." Her speech was slurred.

"Don't move. What kind of injuries have you sustained?" He was steady.

"Daddy, I can't feel my legs and my head hurts really bad."

He had Ida call for an ambulance, give their precise location, and describe her injuries. He also asked if there were a doctor among them. When no one answered, he remembered GG. He asked Ida to alert GG as well that Patty would need medical attention in case the ambulance was delayed.

Then to Patty, "We'll take care of you, darling. Don't move. Try not to worry. We have lots of help. There's also a doctor here."

"Yes, Sir. Thank you."

He then gestured for Ned to come closer to him and handed him the bullhorn.

"Patty. It's Ned. Hi, Baby."

"Hi, Honey."

"Just take it easy. We're getting you out, OK?" Cradling Rosie in one arm and holding the bullhorn in the other, he wanted to free his hands to help with the rescue. He gave Rosie a quick kiss on her snout, rubbed under one of her floppy ears, and told her that she was a good girl before handing her off to a volunteer. He asked the volunteer to place Rosie gently back in her padded wheelbarrow and drive her to Dr. Pete's veterinary hospital.

They tossed the wreckage from the top of the pile, lifting computers, chairs, and tables. They tossed hundreds of books, countless cinder blocks that must have weighed 35-40 pounds each, huge shards of glass, and 2x4 ceiling tiles. The exhumation took a couple of hours and they reached her just at daybreak.

Rev. Harris stretched and noticed the sun beginning to peek over the mountains behind the east wing. It looked like the picture on Patty's retirement invitation. He gazed at it in awe and said so softly that no one else could hear him, "Thank you. We have a resurrection at sunrise and I thank you."

17: Resurrection

Patty was in a peculiar position, facing downward with her knees tucked under her sides and her lower legs pointed away from her body. Her legs were surely broken. Curled over forward with her head touching the ground, her arms were upward and wrapped around her head. One might presume that she had dropped to her knees to pray, ducked and covered to protect her head from falling debris, and then the weight of the wreckage pressed her downward.

Her hands were cut so badly that the rescuers thought that accounted for the blood surrounding her head. After gently lowering her arms, however, they realized there was a large shard of metal, a blade of some sort, lodged in her head.

GG wouldn't leave Lewis' side, so he was on the phone, Skyping, with Ned. He cautioned them not to move her anymore because that could cause further injury. He told them that it was better to have the paramedics lift her from the ground. He also told Ned to continue to talk to her and try to keep her alert.

The sounds of the ambulance sirens gave relief to all of them. After only a few minutes that felt like an eternity, her medical help had arrived.

Rev. Harris began to brief the first responders on Patty's identity and when one of them interrupted him. "We know Patty."

The same paramedic then kneeled close to Patty and said to the one with the clipboard, "traumatic brain injury; object pierced the skull and entered brain tissue; periods of unconsciousness; possible bilateral lower leg fractures; multiple cuts to hands."

The large pile of debris prevented rolling the stretcher to her and they didn't have time to clear a path. They had six volunteers bring the stretcher to her side and hold it steady while four of them lifted her onto it. A small town with limited resources, they did not have a scoop stretcher, one that would allow securely lifting her with minimal personnel. The most secure way they could put her on the stretcher was to use a vertical lift with four of them.

The leading paramedic announced to the others that they would do a "simple lift," knowing that Ned and the other medics were familiar because they had completed Search and Rescue Training together. He stepped over Patty and with one knee down and one knee up, gently lifted her forehead from the ground and rested her face in the palm of his hand. His other hand was centered on her chest just beneath her collarbone.

The second medic stepped over Patty and lifted her elbows into the palms of his hands, first his left and then his right. They were explaining to Patty each step as they lifted.

Ned told Rev. Harris to watch him lift her lower body on her right side so he could repeat it on her left side. Careful not to straighten her leg, Ned held her right ankle in his left hand and then slid that same hand up to her knee. Her lower leg was resting on his left forearm. He stretched his right arm under her pelvis to Rev. Harris so that they could lock hands.

Following Ned's demonstration, Rev. Harris secured her lower left leg from the ankle to the knee and then stretched his other arm underneath her and locked hands with Ned.

Maintaining the exact position in which they found her, the chief then cautioned them of the risk of injury to themselves as carriers, especially of their lumbar backs. To avoid an injury, he instructed them to push upward with their quadriceps and try to keep their backs straight, on his count. He also told them to keep their feet steady and asked if everyone were ready to lift "on three."

On the order of the chief, they lifted Patty from the ground. The volunteers who were holding the stretcher slid it underneath her and held it steady while the lead paramedic gave step-by-step instructions for putting her down on it. Ned first and then Rev. Harris. The other paramedic was next. The chief continued to hold her head, neck and chest steady as he lowered them on the stretcher. They applied a neck brace for stabilization.

They had taken maximum care to avoid worsening her unstable trauma. Her head, neck, and chest axis was kept straight to protect her spine. They kept her body stable with no movement of her legs and feet during the lift.

They didn't roll her over because of her lower body injuries and, obviously, the impaled object in her head. She was faced down on the stretcher in the same froglike position in which they had found her on the ground and she was strapped down at her shoulders and pelvis.

All ten of them lifted her stretcher up into the ambulance. One paramedic called ahead to the hospital to let them know that the casualty had been rescued and was en route. He would drive and the other would ride with her, keeping her steady. Ned rode with her as well. Rev. Harris would drive over to the tent to update Evelyn and Estelle who were still helping GG attend to Lewis.

Just as Rev. Harris started the truck, a second ambulance arrived. Thinking it was a mistake, he waited for it to stop so he could send them away. He was alarmed when they explained to him that they were not there for Patty. There had been another request for an emergency response. He offered to lead them to the tent on the other side of the campus.

The helicopter was still hovering, but their services were no longer needed. Patty had been rescued and, although there was another medical crisis, the sun had arisen so there was no need for their illumination. Rev. Harris would have dismissed them, but thought it best to wait and see what the situation was on the other side of campus. They were continuing their live broadcast.

Ida was outside of the tent trying to make sense of the past 24 hours. The earthquake and power outage, bear attack and rescue, discovery of the family's secrets, Patty's all-night search and rescue, and now Lewis' decline was just too much for her to endure. These were all traumatic circumstances. One of them alone would have been have been a challenge for the bravest person to withstand. The amalgamation of them was simply unbearable.

She noticed the emotional meltdown first in Evelyn, whose mood was swinging like a pendulum. She was ecstatic that Patty was located, but horrified at her condition. At the same time, she was glad that Lewis was with them, but it was too painful to witness his illness and watch him decline. While Evelyn and Ida had not discussed it, she could tell from her interactions with Estelle that they knew they were sisters.

Speaking of Estelle, Ida noticed that she was preoccupied. Whenever someone spoke, they seemed to break her train of thought. Also thrilled that Patty was on her way to receive medical attention, but worried about Lewis, Estelle had so many questions. *Are GG and Lewis a couple? Was it a mere coincidence that they were both coming to the valley this weekend? What happened between her parents that caused them to separate their twin daughters? Had her bond with Patty for the past 20 years been by chance?*

By the time Rev. Harris drove up in the truck, Ida had stepped outside the tent for fresh air. Hunched over with her hands resting on her knees, she was exhausted and weak. She hadn't eaten since the chili when she first arrived the previous afternoon. She couldn't relax because her body felt tense. She was depleted.

Rev. Harris walked up to her and kindly said, "You've done well, Ida. Well done." Once inside the tent, he met Evelyn and Estelle who were glad to see the red flashing lights of the ambulance. He looked at them and then at GG who was sitting up on his cot next to Lewis. Not speaking, he stepped aside for the paramedics to enter.

GG asked them where they would take Lewis and they told him it was the nearest hospital. It was small and overwhelmed with patients from the power outages and earthquake and those injured at the wine festival. The street lights out had caused several car accidents. The earthquake had instigated injuries of hikers and tourists who were roaming the mountains, those meandering the walkways of the Luray Caverns, and countless slip-and-fall incidents in houses. The hospital staff was working diligently to care for each patient, but it could be several hours before Lewis received care.

Estelle was troubled. They had just transported Patty in critical condition. The medics explained that Patty was carried to a trauma center. Lewis' illness, while serious, would not meet the criteria for a specialty center.

Listening in on their exchange, Ida called up to the helicopter. The journalists were still taking pictures and videos, and likely streaming live to the news station. She explained that their family needed one more favor and then handed her phone to GG.

"Where does he need to go?" they asked him.

"Manhattan Acute Care Center. I'm on staff there and so is my brother, Harry. I can make the arrangements."

The journalist and her pilot looked at one another in agreement and without hesitation. One said, "We are not supposed to do this, but under the circumstances, sure, we'll take him."

GG assured Estelle, "Auntie E, I'll call ahead and have Harry prepare for our arrival." Then to Rev. and Mrs. Harris, "I will keep you updated."

Rev. Harris nodded, but did not speak. Evelyn gave Lewis, who was unconscious, a tearful farewell, "Hang in there, my sweet boy. We'll come see you as soon as we return to New York." Estelle and Ida chimed in on his send-off as well with hugs and kisses and quick prayers for wellness.

Still refusing to leave Lewis' side, GG flew in the helicopter with him, holding his hand the entire time. He'd work out the details later of retrieving his car from Patty's house, adjusting his work schedule, and whatever other loose ends remained.

18: Hospital in New York

The flight distance was approximately 350 miles, so they would arrive in about 90 minutes. Although they were not licensed to transport medical patients, they had been participating in the Harris' family emergency for several hours and felt compelled to assist with one more favor. There would be repercussions from their management team as well as financial consequences for their decisions, but Lewis' life, in their opinion, was well worth it.

There would also be legal ramifications. Lewis had rights. He had the right to refuse the form of transportation for any reason; the right to know the risks and benefits of the treatments received on the helicopter; and the right to know the safety hazards of flying.

When he fell asleep, he was with his family. When he awakened, he would not be. The sudden removal from the comfort of his family could be disturbing. He had not yet reunited with Patty and the psychological effects could be severe.

The challenges were not few. There was limited space and, aside from the fatigued GG, there was no medical crew to help care for Lewis. The noise from the rotor blades made it difficult for GG to listen to his lungs or hear the warning alarms from his medical monitors. The helicopter sounds also drowned out sounds of Lewis' moans of pain that signaled to GG when his morphine boost needed to be administered.

Despite all those considerations, GG knew that Lewis was critically ill and much more likely to receive treatment and care at the

MACC than he would set aside, waiting to be triaged at an already overwhelmed, small local hospital. The risks were real, but did not outweigh his chances for surviving a little while longer. The advantage of this helicopter flight over an ambulance ride in the valley would be both the speed at which Lewis arrived at the hospital as well as the quality of the emergency medical team awaiting his arrival.

In just under an hour and a half, the hospital's helipad was in view on the rooftop of the skyscraper. The transport had been smooth. There were no storms or strong winds. There were no air traffic control conflicts, no problems with location identifiers or landing restrictions, no drastic changes in Lewis' condition. Within minutes, they made a perfect landing on the roof of the hospital. The pilot remarked that it was as if something had prepared the way for them and it provided completely unobstructed transport. It had all worked together for their good.

Harry, accompanied by three EMTs, met them at the helipad. It had a dedicated rapid-access lift which could transfer an emergency patient from the helicopter directly into the Emergency Department within minutes.

Lewis' medical records were already in the hospital's patient portal from the biopsy earlier that week. GG repeated for the EMTs' benefit, as Harry was already fully aware, that Lewis' Durable Medical Power of Attorney was also on file there. It clearly stated that if Lewis became incapacitated and unable to handle matters on his own or participate in treatment decisions, then GG would serve as his patient advocate. He had given GG the legal authority to make decisions regarding his care, custody, and medical treatment.

The day they executed that agreement had been emotional for both of them. They were forced to discuss Lewis' preferences for surgery, therapeutic treatments, and life sustaining treatments such as artificial nutrition and hydration. It released from liability anyone who implemented the decisions that GG made to honor his wishes.

He had Stage IV non-small cell lung cancer. It had metastasized throughout his body, was present in his lymph nodes, and affected his liver, bones, and brain. Lewis was aware.

***

GG had explained it in his office before the trip to Shenandoah. "Lung cancers can spread when cells break off from the tumor and travel through the bloodstream or the lymphatics to distant regions of your body and then grow. That process is called metastasis. Your primary lung cancer has spread, metastatic to lymph nodes, liver, bone, and your brain. Lewis, that explains your swollen glands and sore throat, the pain and weakness in your legs, loss of balance and coordination, loss of appetite, and nausea."

"Is it curable?"

"It's not curable, but it is treatable. There are treatments that can help with survival and the symptoms."

"With those treatments, what's my expectancy?"

"We have the opinions of several oncologists. The best are here on staff, Lewis. Treatment is available."

"How long?"

"With treatment, weeks. Maybe a couple of months."

"Could I go to my sister's retirement party?"

"I'm afraid not. We'd need to admit you for this type of treatment."

"I'll pass."

"Lewis, it could give you more time."

"I'm good."

***

Harry did not have to ask why GG was taking such extreme measures to help Lewis. It was obvious that he cared. The Medical PoA was accompanied by another document, a DNR (Do Not Resuscitate) or "no code." It is another legal order written to withhold cardiopulmonary resuscitation (CPR) or advanced cardiac life support (ACLS), in respect of a patient's wishes in case his heart stopped or he stopped breathing. Lewis had signed them all.

It would have been unusual, unprofessional, and unethical for a doctor to become involved with a patient. GG was fully aware, but there was a bond with him, immediate and inexplicable. That evening at the wedding was not the first time they'd met. Lewis had been the photographer of choice among GG's family and friends for many years. He was preferred and requested for their weddings, Bar Mitzvah and Bat Mitzvah celebrations, business events, birthday festivities, and anniversary parties.

Love at first sight might not be a stretch. GG had a formed a habit of asking whom the photographer would be when deciding on his RSVP for some of those invitations. He might have declined some of them except for the opportunity to watch Lewis at his craft.

GG noticed Lewis long before the night he approached but didn't have the nerve to introduce himself. He had imagined someone as handsome and stylish and talented as Lewis would never give him the time of day. Little did he know how much Lewis would have appreciated his company.

Perhaps it was fate that brought them together that evening. Whatever the case, he was grateful for every moment, sick or healthy, lucid or unconscious, that he could spend with Lewis.

The helicopter journalists bid an emotional farewell to GG and Lewis before returning to Virginia. They also asked GG to let Lewis know, when he awakened, that they had taken the liberty of completing his online photo journal. They added two chapters to it.

Lewis' care, rather than therapeutic or remedial, was more like hospice. He received supportive care in the final phase of his terminal illness. The focus was on his comfort and quality of life, rather than a cure or treatment. The goal was to enable him to be comfortable and free of pain so that he lived his remaining time as fully as possible.

Harry was there to provide his brother emotional support. The hospital staff knew them and offered to sit with Lewis so GG could get away for a small break, but he declined. The hospital clergy had come by to discuss their spiritual needs. While their religious beliefs differed greatly, one Jewish and the other Protestant, they both believed in God—the same God.

Lewis received enough drugs to control his pain and manage his other symptoms. By that afternoon, he was relaxed and becoming more alert. As soon as he opened his eyes and focused, he saw GG sitting at his beside, holding his hand, and slouched over, sleeping soundly. Looking around his hospital room, he quickly figured out where he was and how he got there.

Lewis knew that GG must be exhausted and wanted him to rest, so Lewis did not disturb him. He marveled at how thoughtful and selfless and GG had been. *Is this what unconditional love feels like?* he thought. *Why would someone give so much of himself to someone who has so little to offer? How could a doctor as successful and handsome as GG be so attentive to a dying man, especially one whom he just met?*

Lewis looked up at the television and a breaking news caption was scrolling across the bottom of the screen, "Woman rescued from collapsed college building in Virginia."

"Thank you, God! Patty! They saved Patty!"

GG woke at his shrill exclamation. "Yes. They saved her. She's alive, Lewis."

"Where is she?"

"She's in the hospital. The ambulance left with her just before we transported you here."

"My sister is alive."

"Yes, and she'll see all the pictures."

"My pictures?"

"They're all in your online photo journal. Would you like to see them? There's a surprise at the end for you."

GG texted his friend in the hospital's Information Technology department and asked if he could do the thing GG had seen him do for another patient. Within minutes, the guy was in Lewis' private room, had synchronized GG's cellphone to the television, and they were viewing Lewis' photo journal on the TV.

The first chapter opened with the sights and scenery on their road trip. There was a chapter of photos of Patty's house in the mountains. At that point, GG noted, "too bad you didn't get the bear. No one will believe my bear story when I tell it." They laughed.

They advanced through the next few chapters slowly and quietly. He seemed to be studying the pictures, appreciating all the details of the story. His was the last chapter on the field, but there were more. The journalists had completed the chapter of Patty's rescue. He saw his sister excavated from a collapsed building and then lifted onto a stretcher and into the ambulance. He was overjoyed that she was alive.

There was a final chapter. The journalists had created it and named it "Adoration." They didn't know any of the personal details of Lewis' and GG's relationship, so they let the pictures tell the story. There were pictures of GG pushing the wheelchair and carrying equipment, resting next to Lewis in the tent, communicating with his family, and caring for him on the helicopter. The last picture was of their hands, just their hands, one clasping the other.

Lewis could not hold back his emotions. "GG, life without love has been so lonely. Thank you for loving me."

"The pleasure has been all mine. Thank you for sharing this chapter with me."

"I had hoped for this. I'm only sorry that we don't have more time."

"Me too, but I'll never forget you or what we share. I'll cherish every minute."

With labored breathing, "May I ask one more favor?"

"Sure."

"After I fall asleep this time ...," and he looked over his right shoulder at the machines, including the ventilator that had been brought in while they were looking at pictures, but not yet connected to him. He then looked back at GG and shook his head.

"Yes. I know."

19: Hospital in Shenandoah Valley

Patty's ambulance reached the trauma center in a matter of minutes and the medical team was prepared for her arrival. Ned was still with her. She was carried directly to an operating room. Her surgical team first would remove the impaled object from her head. Depending on how she endured that operation, they might set her legs while she was still under anesthesia. They planned to set the bones in her legs, pulling the broken ends back together and then applying a cast to each.

After a hurried conversation with the neurosurgeon who was moving quickly to get to Patty, a nurse suggested Ned rest in a waiting room. "Someone will come out periodically to update you on the progress," she assured him.

Rev. Harris and Evelyn had followed in Ned's truck. Instead of lingering in the hospital waiting room, Evelyn preferred the privacy of the truck. If someone could come out there to update them, she'd appreciate it. Ned agreed. He could come to get them when there was news.

Rev. Harris reclined the driver's seat so that his head tilted back. Evelyn leaned across the console between the two seats so that her head rested on his shoulder. It had been more than 24 hours since they'd rested. She decided that when they were refreshed and had updates on both Patty and Lewis, she wanted to tell her husband about her family discovery.

Estelle and Ida had followed them in Estelle's car. They waited inside in the waiting room with Ned. They also had matters on their hearts that they needed to discuss, but were physically and emotionally drained. They were also worried about Patty and Lewis.

The first surgery, the most critical, addressed her head ordeal. It's not surprising that this type of injury is associated with a high mortality rate. Only one-third of people with penetrating head trauma survive long enough to arrive at a hospital. Patty's survival that long had been a miracle.

The good news was that although the metal scrap had lodged six inches through her skull, she survived the four-hour operation to remove it. The surgeon explained that she came dangerously close to fatality because the object lodged within millimeters of a major artery.

They would have to wait until she was awake to determine whether or not there were cerebral contusions and lacerations, intracranial hematomas, pseudoaneurysms, and arteriovenous fistulas. At the moment, she was comatose.

The report was overwhelming for Ida and Estelle who both began to cry. Ned wrapped an arm around each of them, holding them close to console them, but also to keep himself calm. Evelyn's legs weakened with the news and she leaned against Rev. Harris for support. The rock that he was, he did not falter. With not even the slightest hesitation, and the steadiest of tones, he asked the surgeon, "What's next?"

The doctor, appreciating his lack of emotion, answered him, "they will proceed with the operations for her legs."

Rev. Harris's next question was only one word, "They?"

"Yes, the orthopedic surgeons. I imagine they will likely take another few hours."

Her family was still huddled to receive the updates on Patty when GG called Estelle.

"Auntie E, are you with Lewis' parents?"

"Yes, Baby. We're all here." She reached for Evelyn's hand and looked up to Rev. Harris and put her phone audio on speaker.

"I have very sad news."

"Oh no." Squeezing Evelyn's hand, she began to sob. Unable to speak, she handed her phone to Rev. Harris, the only one of them who maintained composure.

GG continued, "I'm sorry to have to tell you this, Auntie E. Lewis is gone."

"When?" Rev. Harris asked.

Not totally expecting to hear that voice, but not really surprised either, he answered, "A few minutes ago."

"You were with him?"

"Yes, Sir. I still am."

"Very well."

"How's Patty?"

"Critical."

"Right. OK. Please have Auntie E call me back when she's ready to talk."

Rev. Harris ended the call.

Ned led Estelle and Ida to a sofa in the corner. The three of them, never losing their embrace, wept. They didn't speak. There was nothing to say. No one tried to console the others. The embrace was all the consolation they could muster.

Rev. Harris walked his wife to a single chair by the window. She sat, dropped her face into her hands, and bawled. They didn't speak either. He stood beside her chair, facing the window with his back to everyone in the room. A strong figure, statue-like, silent and motionless, he looked out the window, upward toward the sun.

The next few hours seemed to drag on forever. Grieving the loss of Lewis and accepting the reality of his passing was unbearable. They had just been with him a few hours prior. Estelle suggested that, given Patty's condition, they might hold Lewis' memorial service in

Shenandoah. She assured Evelyn that she would help with all the arrangements.

Waiting for Patty to come out of her second set of operations was torture. There had been no updates since they had spoken with her neurosurgeon.

The Goodleafs arrived and, as was typical for them, brought provisions for the family. Mr. Goodleaf was pulling a hand truck with crates and boxes stacked on them. Mrs. Goodleaf set up a folding table and spread a cloth over it. She plugged in her coffee urn and started the brew. She had warmed venison stew from their freezer and baked fresh bread. After plugging in the crockpot with the stew, she sliced the bread for them and arranged it on a platter. According to Mrs. Goodleaf, no bread would be fit to eat without her assortment of homemade spreads and that included a jar each of apple butter, strawberry jam, and pear preserves. In another basket, she provided an ample heap of her prize-winning apple pastries.

Mr. Goodleaf, without formality, not assembling everyone or holding hands, asked a blessing over the food. "Dear God. Thank you for this food. Please bless it as nourishment for the bodies of all who partake. Amen."

Everyone in the room agreed with "Amen."

They were beginning to serve themselves when, finally, another doctor entered the waiting room. His news was not as discouraging as that of the first surgeon. They had completed operations on both of Patty's legs and he remarked that "her legs were incredibly strong, a runner's legs." He even went so far as to compare them to "a racehorse." He also felt confident that, apart from the neurological distresses, there was no reason to doubt that she would regain use of her legs. He reiterated, however, that because she remained in a coma, the next several hours would be crucial to her recovery.

"Can I see her?" Evelyn asked softly.

"Briefly, yes. Once she's in a recovery room, we will send someone for you."

After another hour or so passed, an attendant came into the waiting room. "Patricia Harris. Are you the family of Patricia Harris?"

Evelyn stood, "Yes. I'm her mother."

"Ma'am, you can see her now, but we ask that you keep your visit very brief and only one person at a time, please."

"Of course." She followed him down the corridor.

She gasped when she entered Patty's recovery room. Her legs were suspended in the air with cables and slings. They were casted and bandaged from her waist down, only revealing her toes. Her arms lay to her sides and both her hands were bandaged. Her head was completely wrapped in medical gauze and it was turned to one side in a stabilizer. The massive heap of gauze in the back protected the area where the metal shard had been removed.

Also, there were tubes: down her throat, in her nose, and in both her arms. From underneath her blanket, there were more, including catheters for drainage.

Evelyn leaned over to Patty's ear and whispered, hoping she could hear her. "Patricia, I'm here dear. You survived. You're strong and you're a survivor. I love you."

As Evelyn exited the recovery room, Rev. Harris was waiting just outside the door. He held her and helped her back to the waiting room, but he did not go inside Patty's room. He couldn't. He motioned for Ned to go next while he stayed with the ladies.

Ned, with trembling hands and puffy eyes, gently held her hand. He spoke to her as well, "Patty, it's Ned, Baby. I'm here. You were in an accident and you got hurt, but you made it out. You're in the hospital and we're here. We're pulling for you. I need you to wake up. Please. Wake up so we can pick out your ring, set our date, and finally share our lives. I love you so much!"

Rev. Harris then sent Ida and Estelle together to see Patty. He wanted Ned to stay with Evelyn, while he went for a walk.

"Patty, it's Ida. Hey, girl. You gave us all quite a scare. We thought we had lost you. I'm so glad you're here, Patty. You're the best fried I've ever had. You're the sister I never had. I love you, Pat and I'll be here when you wake up, OK?" Moving to the other side of the bed so that Estelle could face Patty, Ida couldn't stop crying.

"Patty, it's Estelle. Hi, Baby. I knew you'd survive. I knew it. You're a survivor. I have so much to tell you. You won't believe what we discovered. Family secrets, Patty. Deep family secrets, but we don't have to talk about that right now. You just rest, Baby. We'll have plenty of time to talk later. I love you, Patty."

When they returned to the room, the Goodleafs were still fussing over the family, making sure everyone had food and drink and blankets. Satisfied that everyone was settled in, Rev. Harris decided it was his turn to go to her room.

A man of steel, he walked steadily down the corridor. With his head up, shoulders back, arms at his side, he walked with a cadence. When he reached her room, on the last step he transferred his weight to his forward foot then turned 180°, pivoting to her door. He stood there, looking through the small window on the door that was just at his eye level.

A nurse came up beside him and offered, "Sir, I can go in with you if you'd like."

Not losing sight of Patty, not turning his head to look at the nurse, "No. Thank you."

He peered through the window and he could see his daughter lying there, but he did not go inside her room. He couldn't.

20: Prayer

Rev. Harris marched up to the nurses' station and asked for directions to the hospital chapel.

"We can have the chaplain come to you, Sir. If we call him, he will gladly come to you."

"I did not ask for a chaplain. I asked for the chapel."

"Yes, of course." She pulled up a copy of the hospital map on a mobile tablet and pointed to the chapel. "I can print this map for you."

"That's not necessary. I've got it. Thank you." He turned and walked away in his rhythmic cadence.

He navigated the hospital like he'd worked there for years. The turns, corridors, elevators, and double doors were no challenge to him at all. In a matter of minutes, he had approached a sign with an arrow, "Chapel, this way."

He was relieved that the room was empty. There was something about a church or church-like setting that soothed him. Back home he could sit in his empty church for hours and enjoy the solitude.

He exhaled when he entered the quaint chapel. There were two sets of pews with seven rows each—one set on either side of the room. Their placement created an aisle down the center of the room. There was no lighting above the pews and his eyes were drawn to the front, center of the room. To the left was one stained glass window and a tall plant beside it in the corner. To the right, in the corner, was a set of heavy wooden double doors that probably led back to an office. There was a tall plant beside those doors, matching the one across the room. In the center, there were three recessed lights, providing the only lighting in the room.

On the wall, centered, was an enormous crucifix—the large statement piece in the room. On a different day, under other circumstances, he would have debated the philosophy of the crucifix. His beliefs would lean more toward the representation of a cross than a crucifix. *But, not today. Not now.*

Beneath the crucifix was a podium, not unlike the podium where he delivered his Sunday sermons. To the left of that podium was a single chair. Another detail he would have questioned because only the ordained belonged in the pulpit, *but not today.*

He made his way down the aisle and his first inclination was to stand behind the pulpit. He resisted that impulse and, instead, sat on the front pew.

He was just about to pray when the chaplain entered from behind the double doors. "Hello."

"I prefer to be alone."

"I understand…"

Before the chaplain could finish his statement, he justified. "I was a chaplain. I am a pastor. I know how this works. I prefer to be alone."

"I see. Well, if you need anything…"

"I need the doors locked so I won't be interrupted again."

"Of course." The chaplain left the room.

***

Father God, I thank you for every blessing in my life. You've been kind and merciful and gracious. Thank you for your son, Jesus. Thank you for your blessed Holy Spirit.

Thank you for hearing and answering prayers. When I was a young boy and my father was abusive to my mother, I wondered where you were and if you cared. Well, that was until I asked you for protection and you provided it. Then I asked you for the courage to stand up to him and you gave it to me. When I asked you for a safe haven, you sent us to live with my grandparents, where he could never harm us again. You answered my every call. Thank you. I vowed in return to protect the women in my life from harm and danger. I've tried my best.

Father, you've brought me through an honorable military career, 50 years of marriage to a wonderful woman, and fatherhood of two amazing children. Thank you. Where I've gone wrong with them, please forgive me.

I come now, Lord, not to question your will, but to bring you my broken heart. You blessed us with Patrick, Jr., and now you've called him home. He is my son, my namesake. I know that you know the pain of losing a son, but this is new for me. Is there no pain like outliving your child? I have to bury my son and that feels out of order.

I wanted the best for him and guided him the way I thought he should go. He was obedient, but he was not happy. He only had a few short hours to live out his dream. I witnessed it. I saw his joy. I wish he'd had more time to live his passion, but I do thank you for granting him the experience.

It did not surprise me that my son never married. I knew for years who he was. He knew that I knew. He also knew that if he forced me to choose between supporting his lifestyle and standing firm on your Word, that I'd choose you, Father. I will always choose you. Patrick was such a loving son that he never presented the option, never required me to choose. He put his love for me and respect for our relationship before his own happiness. I am grateful that, although it was only for a short period of time, he was able to experience love and adoration. Thank you for allowing him to live it and me to witness it.

Father, I thank you for my Evelyn. She has been a loving and dutiful wife. She has granted my every wish and denied me nothing. Honoring our marriage, even when she vehemently disagrees with my decisions, has always been her priority. She chooses me every time, over everything else, including our own children.

She's hurting. She's scared. She's tired, and I've protected her to the best of my ability. Many years ago, I promised her father that I'd keep his family secret and I did. She knows now. I know that she knows. I can't imagine the pain she will feel when she learns that I've known all along. I need you to help her understand that I was shielding her. He was a good man and he had his reason for making the decisions that he made and he trusted me to safeguard it. Thank you for allowing me to be her husband. Please forgive me for where I've fallen short with her.

I pray that Ned will be that kind of husband to Patricia. He's smart and strong and he loves her. Thank you for sending her someone who loves her so much. Forgive me for driving a wedge between them years ago.

Thank you for Estelle. She knows also. I can tell. I was afraid it would have come out sooner, but it's been 20 years since Patricia moved here. Estelle has loved her as only an aunt, a mother's twin, could love her niece. I've never had to worry about Patricia because I knew that Estelle was here for her. It's been a weight on my soul to keep that secret for twenty years. I thank you for their love and I thank you for relieving me of the burden.

Father, Ida is the closest Patricia has to a sister. She's dependable. She's a good person. She's a good friend. Thank you for placing her in our lives.

Now, God, Patricia. My Patricia. You said not to be anxious about anything, but I confess that I'm anxious right now. I'm worried. I'm fearful. I'm afraid. I've lost one child today. Please God, don't take my other one. I don't know that I could be strong enough to help Evelyn through it. I don't know that I'm strong enough to survive it.

You said to come to you in every situation, so here I am. You said to pray and petition you, so here I am. You said to come to you with thanksgiving and here I am. I'm thankful for every blessing you've bestowed upon us and especially my Patricia. She was good girl and she grew to become a good woman. She's a good sister, friend, niece, and daughter. She's a good teacher and neighbor. She's a good person and I thank you for every minute of her life.

You said to present my requests to you. I am requesting, Father, that you spare my little girl. Heal her. I know you can. Restore her. I know you're able. Touch her with your mighty hand and mend her everywhere she's broken. Recondition her and rebuild her from the inside out. I believe you will. Father, while she lies there, nearly lifeless, have your spirit breathe life into her. Do not leave her comfortless, but please send a band of angels to camp out in her room and watch over her. I can't see you, but I know you're here and I hope you'll answer. I'm asking you Father, to grant us this miracle. Bless us indeed.

Thank you for the opportunity to come to you, for allowing me to bring my concerns to you. I know that you're a healer. I know that you're a miracle worker. Thank you for the balm in Gilead. Thank you for making the wounded whole. Thank you for the power in heaven that cures a sin-sick soul.

Now, Father, knowing that you have received my thanksgiving and heard my requests, please know this—if what I ask does not align with your will, you are still my God. If you do not see fit to grant my desires, you are still my God. You are Lord of my life. I love you and I honor you and I worship you and I praise you no matter what happens in this place.

You are the Holy One and I adore you. I bow down before you in adoration because you are the Lord of Lords and the King of Kings. You are the great I Am. You are mighty and merciful. If you deny my request because you have greater plans that I know not of, then so be it. You are God, my sovereign master. You reign supreme and I'm honored to be in your presence. My greatest joy is serving you. You are all powerful, all wonderful, and my soul belongs to you. I will bless you at all times, even these, the most difficult. I will sing your praises even in the midst of my sorrow and suffering. How great thou art, My God, how great thou art!

***

He's not sure when he'd done it, but he'd moved from the front pew to the pulpit. He had preached to himself and was singing at the top of his voice,

O Lord my God, when I in awesome wonder,
Consider all the worlds Thy hands have made;
I see the stars, I hear the rolling thunder,
Thy power throughout the universe displayed.

The tears were streaming down his cheeks when he felt someone catch hold of his hand. It was the chaplain, singing with him,

Then sings my soul, my Savior God, to Thee,
How great Thou art! How great Thou art!
Then sings my soul, My Savior God, to Thee,
How great Thou art! How great Thou art!

21: Substance of Things Hoped For

The hospital staff was announcing that visiting hours were over and asking all family members to leave for the evening. Ned asked one of the security officers if he could have a word with him. The officer stepped into the waiting room and closed the door behind him. Only the Harris family remained in the waiting room.

Before Ned could ask if they could stay longer, the officer assured him that it would be OK. They wouldn't be able to go back inside Patty's room that night, but they could walk down to her door and glance through the window. For Evelyn and Estelle, that was good enough. Leaving Patty in the hospital alone that night was too much to ask of them.

The officer was trying to concentrate on his conversation with Ned, but was distracted. Ida, almost 36 hours since she'd dressed and left Manhattan, still had appeal. He was smitten. He made his way over the armchair where she sat and introduced himself. "Hi, I'm Jack Goodleaf."

"Goodleaf?"

"Yes, Ma'am."

"Are you related to Patty's neighbors?"

"Yes. They're my uncle and aunt." He looked down at the wine bottle. "I see you like our product."

"Your product?" She looked at the bottle to read the label, *Goodleaf Vineyard and Cellars.*

Evelyn and Estelle were falling asleep, embracing one another, under a shared blanket. Ned, still drinking coffee, watched the news on the television that was mounted up on the wall when Rev. Harris returned to the waiting room.

"Hello, Sir." Ned had been curious about his whereabouts, but did not question him. "They're all over the news, Lewis and Patty."

Mrs. Goodleaf insisted that Rev. Harris eat and scooped two ladles full of stew in to a bowl. She buttered bread for him and handed him a bottle of water. With red eyes and a lenient posture, he dropped into a chair beside Ned and received it. "It smells delicious."

Responding to the first kind words she'd heard him say, "I hope you enjoy it. The recipe has been in my family for generations. It's Patty's favorite."

Waiting for her to finish speaking, he politely responded, "I'm sure I will. Thank you, and thank you for loving my little girl." He smiled through his tears.

Rev. Harris and Ned were watching the news when a breaking story came on, they were going to broadcast Lewis' photo journal. He had done it. Posthumously but, nevertheless, he had become a famous photojournalist.

The commentators were admiring Lewis' work and how his collection of images told the entire news story of his sister's tragic accident and amazing rescue. It was remarkable journalism.

Rev. Harris thought a gentleman in a few of the photos in the beginning had a striking resemblance to the hospital chaplain, but the slide show moved so quickly that he wasn't sure. He watched in amazement.

After the chapter that showed the building collapse and Patty's parked truck, the next one was named, "My Hero." It opened with a silhouette of his father. Because Lewis was in a wheelchair, he captured an upward view of his father with the evening sky as a backdrop. He appeared larger than life, statuesque. He had captured his physical strength when he was digging the path for the wheelchair; his leadership when directing the squads he'd formed; and his empty chair because he remained on the field, involved in the search the entire time. The last picture Lewis had taken of his father must have been from the tent and when he looked back toward him. His head was bowed and his hands were clasped. He was determined and prayerful. Rev. Harris was honored. He had no idea that his son had such admiration for him. In his son's eyes, he was a hero.

He was wiping his eyes when Ned thought to give him a little privacy. "Sir, I'm going to walk down to Patty's room. I'll be back soon."

"Sure," was all he could respond.

When he turned onto the acute care unit, there was activity in Patty's room. Two people were hurrying a cart with a machine into her room. A red light was flashing over her doorway. People were running and rushing and Ned froze. He wanted to move, but his legs wouldn't cooperate.

He stood there, petrified. After a couple of minutes passed, he felt someone holding his hand and he could hear him. The chaplain was whispering the 23rd Psalm:

The Lord is my shepherd; I shall not want.

He maketh me to lie down in green pastures: he leadeth me beside the still waters.

He restoreth my soul: he leadeth me in the paths of righteousness for his name's sake.

Yea, though I walk through the valley of the shadow of death, I will fear no evil: for thou art with me; thy rod and thy staff they comfort me.

Thou preparest a table before me in the presence of mine enemies: thou anointest my head with oil; my cup runneth over.

Surely goodness and mercy shall follow me all the days of my life: and I will dwell in the house of the Lord forever.

Ned was grateful for that prayer and repeated parts of it, "I shall not want;" "He restoreth my soul;" "Surely goodness and mercy shall follow me." He was beginning to calm down and regain the feeling in his legs again when Rev. Harris approached and recognized the chaplain.

"Thank you, Chaplain."

"My pleasure."

Then to Ned, "Are you OK, Son?"

"I think so, Sir." Then looking back, "Is he the chaplain?"

"Yes."

"How do you know him?"

"We met in the chapel." Then, changing the subject, "Let's go back to the waiting room so they can work. She'll be fine."

Officer Goodleaf covered Ida with a blanket when she fell asleep, slipped his business card into her purse, and eased out of the room. The sisters were still asleep on the sofa. The Greenleafs were asleep as well, sharing a rollaway bed on the other side of the room.

Ned thought he detected disappointment in Rev. Harris when he looked up at the television and they had moved on to another news story. "Sir, I'm sure you can view the photos from your cellphone. I can show you how."

"I'd appreciate that."

Ned downloaded Lewis' photo journal to Rev. Harris' phone and explained that he had copies saved that he could view with or without an internet connection, as often as he wanted.

"Thank you, Son."

"You're welcome, Rev. Harris."

"Ned, you can call me Dad. After all, you're going to be family soon, right?"

"Yes, Sir. Dad." He smiled.

It was not long before they fell asleep, too. Each in a separate chair, slouched over, their bodies had acknowledged that they had been awake for two days, searching, digging, hoping, and praying. No one else came into the waiting room that night. They were able to rest in peace.

The next morning, as soon as the sun peeped over the mountains, Rev. Harris' eyes opened. He walked over to the windows and looked upward. As was his morning ritual, he recited the same passage aloud, "It is of the Lord's mercies that we are not consumed, because his compassions fail not. They are new every morning: great is thy faithfulness."

Just then a nurse came in to tell the family that the neurosurgeon was with Patty and would be in soon to update them. Rev. Harris woke them all up so they'd be ready to receive news.

By the time they were alert, he was there.

"Good Sunday morning, family. We knew that the first night would be the most critical. We will not know if there's permanent neurological damage for a while. We have many tests to run and she has a long road ahead of her. The good news, however, is that she has awakened. She is alert and she is responsive."

"She's awake!" Evelyn exclaimed. Forgetting to seek her husband's permission she asked, "Can we see her?"

"You may, but please keep it brief."

Evelyn and Estelle went first and passed a nurse on their way out of the waiting room. The nurse wanted to know if the family would like to see the chaplain.

"Thank you," Rev. Harris answered, "but we saw him last night."

"The chaplain?"

"Yes, I saw him in the chapel and then again in the hallway with Ned a little later."

"That's not possible."

"Pardon?"

"The chaplain was not on duty. He's been on call this weekend, available to come in if needed. We didn't call him in, Sir. You asked us not to call him."

Rev. Harris and Ned looked at one another, each knowing what the other had seen.

Acknowledgements

This book would not have been possible without the anointing of God. "I thank him who has enabled me, trusted me, and appointed me to do his work" (1 Tim1:12). I also thank him for confirming through both Pastor Danell Perkins and Prophetess Deborah Webb that this is my assignment, to write books that draw people closer to God.

An entire village supports and encourages me on my journey. From the moment that I answered my calling, family and friends have been reassuring me of their enthusiasm and excitement for my work. Thank you sincerely: Isaac Spencer, Jr; Gail Whitaker; Sherry McNeil, Daren Jones, and Edward Harding, Sr., aunts, uncles, cousins, neighbors, students, colleagues, and church members.

About the Author

Dr. Shawn Jones Richmond is an entrepreneur, educator, and now, an author of contemporary fiction and Bible Study workbooks. Her PhD is in Organization and Management and her graduate studies were centered on education and technology.

Recently, she completed another degree program and graduated from a theological seminary. She has been studying, praying, and preparing for this appointed time to use all that God has gifted her, to strengthen families and mend broken connections.

To learn more about Dr. Richmond and her work, visit http://DrShawnRichmond.com, join her mailing list, and connect with her on social media.